All Claims

To Marion & Peto

Best Wishes

Colin

1/1/15

All Claims Great and Small

The Trials and Tribulations of a "Lost" Adjuster

James D Buchanan

© James D Buchanan, 2014

Published by Denise Bowes

A CIP catalogue record for this book is available from the British Library.

ISBN 978-0-9929171-0-4

Book layout and cover design by Clare Brayshaw

Prepared and printed by:

York Publishing Services Ltd
64 Hallfield Road
Layerthorpe
York YO31 7ZQ

Tel: 01904 431213

Website: www.yps-publishing.co.uk

For the wee wifie with the hope that the next 54 years are as good as the first.

Contents

An Old Adjuster

I am an old adjuster with hair iron grey
Me memory's not too bad though I'm 60 today
Or else 62 no...I can't be 64
Well maybe I am but I'm not a day more!
I can reckon it out I was born in mmm – dear me....
Why at that rate I must be turned 73
Oh this confusion it gets me upset
Why, I'm 80 I think I forget.. I forget

I first joined the firm in 1810;
No, that can't be right I wasn't born then!
It was 1903 .... wrong again it was not –
No, that's someone's telephone number I've got.
They gave me a loss to adjust favourably
And sent me by train to the cotton spinning country.
There I met the insured and in some trepidation
I offered him a settlement in full compensation
Now did he consent in a tone of regret,
Or say, "Not enough! " I forget...I forget

Oh well it seems I'm getting old
And not much use at adjusting I'm told
But I just jog along as the days come and go
And wait for the call that is coming I know
And when the final halt comes and I hear the last call
That comes from THE GREATEST ADJUSTER of
all! Then whate'er there is in the past to regret
I'll just hand in my report and hope he'll forget!

Percy Knowles 1897 to 1980
Ex Manager of Teasdale and Harrup,
Manchester

I Did It My Way (Part I)

It was a warm evening in the summer of 1969. I was driving along the A580 in an easterly direction having left the M6 motorway at Junction 23 from where there is a good view of Haydock racecourse. This thoroughfare which links Liverpool, "where the gentlemen live", to Manchester, "where the men live", goes by the fine title of The East Lancashire Road.

My name is James Douglas Buchanan born a Sagittarian on the 16th December 1945 of Scottish parents in Marple, Cheshire but raised in Lancashire where I still live. I am thus a mongrel. A Cheshire Cat with Scottish blood and a robust Lancashire spirit and at the tender age of 23 now finding myself on the way to the fair City of Manchester to attend an after hours job interview for the position of Junior Loss Adjuster at the offices of the old established and well respected firm of Teasdale and Harrup.

I was grateful to The Green Shield Stamp Company in that two weeks ago they had exchanged my several books of their stamps for a "clip on the car window" radio aerial. There were two reasons for my gratitude, firstly, that I did not have to drill a hole in the front wing of my company car to install a traditional aerial (which would have resulted in a severe ear bashing) and secondly, that I could now listen to my battery-powered transistor radio, nestling on the front passenger seat, with some clarity.

In 1969 the majority of cars manufactured did not include a car radio in their specification this being reserved for the luxury models of the day.

The vehicle that I was driving from Preston to Manchester was not mine but was a company car designated for my sole use. It was a brand new red Morris Mini Minor 1000 with registration number TMK 792F rejoicing in the nick-name of Timoshenko.

The car, of which I had been the custodian for just a few months, still held onto that lovely new car smell which was exaggerated by the warmth of the evening.

As I drove through the equally fair City of Salford, nearing my destination, Frank Sinatra was serenading me with the closing lines of his massive hit of the day, My Way, with the words:-

"...... and more ... much more than this ... I did it ... Myyyy Waayyyy."

In The Beginning

Before I reach my destination let me give you some background information, tell you a little about myself and why you find me on the way to a job interview. I already held the position of Trainee Loss Adjuster at a small office in the town of Preston in the County of Lancashire.

I was living on the Fylde Coast with my widowed mother Alice and my younger sister Mary, my elder sister and brother having fled the nest some years before and now both living abroad. Our terraced house was great and overlooked one of the fairways of The Royal Lytham and St Anne's Golf Club where in a few weeks time Tony Jacklin would win the British Open Golf Championship; but I was in a poky wee office in Preston and considered that I "needed a change".

I had worked in Manchester before and was very fond of and familiar with the City. My employers at that time had been The Griffin and Globe Insurance Company Limited whom I joined in 1963 straight from school with my 4 GCE O levels (which of necessity included Maths and English Language) tucked carefully under my arm. My position was that of a clerk in the Fire Claims Department, at the annual salary of £ 350. One of my duties was to instruct loss adjusters to deal with larger more complex claims on behalf of The Griffin and Globe. The system was that the loss adjusting firm would investigate the claim, ensure that there was appropriate cover under the terms and conditions of the policy then agree a settlement and thereafter submit a report to G & G with their recommendations together with a note of their fees and expenses for the work.

I thus became acquainted with several loss adjusters employed by the various firms in the North West of England being occasionally treated to both solid and liquid luncheons by way of a "thank you" for putting work their way.

At that early stage in my career in the insurance industry I lived in Rochdale, Lancashire with my parents John and Alice, my brother George and two sisters, Nancy and Mary. As I have said dad and mum were Scottish born in Perth and Paisley respectively and had made their way down to Manchester by car with two pals in a Morris 8 not long after they were married to start a new job and a new life.

They actually made the journey on Sunday the 3rd September 1939, the day that Neville Chamberlain announced that Great Britain was declaring war against Germany. The family folklore is that they were in a café in Shap village when they heard the news. A very uncertain and scary time for the newly weds.

Dad was an accountant and initially worked for a firm of Chartered Accountants in Spring Gardens, Manchester. One of his duties was to audit the accounts of a cotton spinning company in Rochdale, John Bright and Brothers Ltd, whose offices were opposite Cronkeyshaw Common, off the road to Whitworth. He carried out this audit for a few years and did a good job and was well liked by the senior management of that company.

Sometime later, specifically 1950 when I was four and a half years old, the existing Company Secretary retired from business and dad was offered the job. He accepted enthusiastically having a wife and children to support. There was a pay rise, the use of the original mill owner's splendid house, Rose Hill, and a company car. The big house, gardens, a wooded area and a paddock became a great playground for us children but I recall dad saying to mum a few years later that he missed his colleagues and the buzz of his office life in Manchester.

Life was good for me growing up in Rochdale where I made lots of friends at Greenbank Junior School, the Trinity Presbyterian Church Sunday School and Youth Club, the Rochdale and District Scottish Society (where I became one eighth of a junior Scottish dancing demonstration team) and at Rochdale Grammar School for Boys where I didn't do very well academically but did well socially. Loads of great pals; and the lead guitarist of the school's Shadows style pop group! The truth is that I played on the guitar most weekday evenings, learning new tunes with a view to becoming the next Hank B Marvin, instead of concentrating on my school homework!

Then came an event which turned our family life upside down. Dad, who I knew suffered from angina, wasn't feeling well. The doctor had been called for and she recommended bed rest and said that she would arrange for some tests the following week. In the meantime dad remained in bed whilst the rest of us got on with our daily tasks and pastimes. At noon on Sunday the 31st January 1965 I was asked by mum to take a tray with dad's lunch up to their bedroom. As soon as I walked in I knew that there was something dreadfully wrong. He was obviously in pain and when he saw the food he struggled to say,

"Take it away! Get your mother! "

I ran downstairs shouting for mum but by the time we had rushed back up to the bedroom he was dead, having suffered a heart attack. He was only 55 years of age. I was just nineteen and my wee sister Mary was only eleven.

As mentioned our elder sister Nancy and family and elder brother George were living abroad at the time and of course returned home as soon as possible. Once the funeral had taken place Nancy and George returned to their own lives and the three of us were left to fend for ourselves. I was in shock and the event made me develop great sympathy with young people who lose one or both parents. Little

Mary was a lost soul, she and dad were very close and I had to be strong for her and did my best to comfort her and help her through this terrible time.

I was particularly upset in that I considered that I was just getting to know dad "man to man", so to speak. Being the third born out of four presumably I occupied a quarter of dad's affection for his children, but once Nancy and George had left home, we were able to spend more time together and I grew closer to him. He was well educated and intelligent, had a sense of humour, was very interested in music both classical and popular and was a good pianist. We owned a decent Philco record player and a couple of wireless sets. The house was always filled with music of all types from the likes of, ('Til) I Kissed You by The Everly Brothers, to Fingal's Cave by Felix Mendelssohn.

Thinking back, I reckon that dad hadn't been well for quite a long time, as he always seemed to be tired and short of breath. During the several months before he died he would come home from the office, have his tea and now and again say, "James, do you fancy a run in the car?"

He couldn't walk too far so he enjoyed those evening runs. His company car at the time was a pale blue Wolseley 15/60, registration number YDK 559. The seats were upholstered in pale blue leather and, I recall, the specification included a very smart leather key fob in the same colour.

We would drive through Bacup to Todmorden and then through Mytholmroyd and return on the B6138, "over the tops", to Littleborough and then back home. Dad had paid for the car to be fitted with a radio and on one memorable journey the song, True Love, performed by Bing Crosby and Grace Kelly from the film High Society, was aired. We sang along in harmony,

> "For you and I have a guardian angel
> On high with nothing to do
> But to give to you and to give to me
> Love for ever true...oo
> Love for ever true."

That became dad's song and still brings a lump to my throat when I hear it.

A few weeks after the funeral mum was invited to have a meeting with dad's employers about the future. I said that I wanted to attend being now the man of the house! We had to hand the car back, but before doing so, I removed the radio and speaker, and kept them safe in the hope that mum would at some time be able to buy a car of her own.

There was some life insurance money but not a fortune by any means. Dad dying left us in a bit of a hole because, as I mentioned, a perk of his job was that we were provided with a house and as a new Company Secretary was to be appointed we would have to leave. We were given a reasonable time to arrange this which was appreciated and mum's first thought was to move back across the border to the "auld country". We had many relations living in Scotland and in one way it made sense.

As a family we had become very familiar with the pleasures of day trips to the borough of Lytham St Anne's on Lancashire's Fylde Coast, a combination of two smaller towns, Leafy Lytham and Sandy Saint Anne's-on-the-Sea. The borough was just seven miles south of the "Las Vegas of the North", the brilliant town of Blackpool!

In addition to liking the area one of dad's cousins her husband and family lived in Lytham and they were keen for us to be near to them. Following some serious consideration of the pros and cons of the situation a decision was made and we moved to a new home in Lytham. Mum used the bulk of the Life Insurance money to buy the house outright for £3,750.

At least we now owned the roof over our heads and had chosen a lovely part of the United Kingdom of Great Britain and Northern Ireland in which to live. The Griffin and Globe kindly transferred me to their Preston office, which is a short railway journey from Lytham, where once again I was asking local loss adjusting firms to deal with larger claims on the company's behalf.

After I had been working at the Preston office for sometime a pal of mine called Alan from a locally based loss adjusting firm came into the office one day and gestured for me to come to the counter. He then whispered that I should look at next week's edition of The Post Magazine (an insurance industry weekly publication) as there would be a job advertised in which I might be interested! Alan said that he could "Say no more," winked, and was gone. I didn't have to buy the magazine as a copy was delivered to the office each week.

I was sorting out the daily postal delivery a few days later when I saw the magazine in its cellophane wrapper. I knew it was more than my life was worth to open it and put it as usual with the pile of correspondence designated for the manager, Mr Boyle, a fearsome boss of the old school.

The usual pattern was that Mr Boyle would hang onto it for a couple of days and when he had read it from cover to cover would place it on the coffee table near to the counter in the Reception area of the office.

The day came and I watched from my desk as Mr Boyle plonked the magazine on the table and went back into his office. I felt like Bob Cratchit to his Ebenezer Scrooge as I slowly crept over to the table and removed the publication away from the gaze of the chief clerk and my fellow clerks. Without losing a stride I continued my creep to the lavatory where I made myself comfortable and thumbed the pages frantically to the jobs section. There it was! Alan must be leaving as his job was up for grabs!

"Assistant Loss Adjuster required for the Preston Office of D. Henderson and Sons. Previous experience not essential but some progress in the examinations of The Chartered Insurance Institute would be preferred. Company car. Salary £650 per annum"

"My God! This is a great job! A company car ... and £150 more than my current salary," I said excitedly to the lavatory cubicle door.

I posted my application letter, attended the interview and to my surprise got the job! It was the company car that did it for me. I had pals who were reps for various companies and I was envious of their perk of a company car. It was the one thing that I really wanted. There was no way that I could think of buying one so what better way than this to gain some wheels and a pay rise!

Mr Boyle accepted my resignation but mumbled something about me losing the rights to a non contributory Widows Benefit Scheme or some such nonsense in the mind of a single chap of 20 years of age! I think Mr Boyle was relieved that I was going as it had been my impression that the granting of my transfer to his branch by the Regional Office in Manchester, following dad's untimely death, had put an unwanted financial burden on his "profitability". I certainly wasn't overworked during my several months at the branch.

So it was "Goodbye" to The Griffin and Globe Insurance Company Limited, Insurers of General and Life Assurance business, who had been good to me, and where I made some great friends, and "Hello" to D. Henderson and Sons, Chartered Loss Adjusters.

The first day of my new job included the handing over of the car keys. I was not impressed. The car was a clapped out C registration, maroon coloured, Austin Mini Minor 750cc, with 70,000 miles on the clock! The first time that I drove it was a shock. It made terrible noises and pulled horribly to the left. It was a battle to keep the blooming thing in a straight line. I also noticed that the petrol tank had a slight leak. It was a physical wreck, and I became a nervous wreck!

After a few days of being an unwilling "Hell Driver" I aired my concerns to Mr George Goodall the resident partner (and thus my new boss) and he reluctantly said,

"You'd better take it round to A & N Motors in Avenham Place. We have an account with them. Get them to check it over. Make sure you see Mr Nolan. Tell him I sent you. Don't deal with his assistant. He's not a full shilling."

I did more than that by telling Mr Nolan to, "Do anything that needs to be done!"

I received a phone call from him a couple of days later when the work was complete and walked around to the garage to collect the Mini. After thanking Mr

Nolan I drove the repaired beast away from his back street garage. There was no doubt that he and his mechanic (who in my opinion WAS a full shilling) had done a splendid job as the car drove very well indeed.

A few days later the invoice for the work arrived by post. I became aware that after Mr G had opened the envelope and had started to read the content of the enclosure his complexion turned from it's normal beige to a throbbing purple which enhanced the broken veins in his face! The bill was relatively massive and Mr Goodall was far from impressed!

"Bloomin' heck laddie! I told you to get them to check it out not rebuild the bloody thing. And that's swearing. Yes you've made me swear and I don't swear, do I Miss Merridew?" The last comment being directed to the only other member of staff. There were just the three of us at the Preston Office which I will elaborate upon later. I managed to calm him down and the matter was soon a thing of the past.

As the months rolled along I found that I quite enjoyed the work, especially being paid for driving around the area to reach the claimants' homes, guest houses, farms, shops and small businesses. The Preston Office of Hendersons covered West and East Lancashire and Cumberland so I was often dealing with claims on The Fylde Coast, The Lake District and The Trough of Bowland as well as the more industrialized towns such as the Accrington, Blackburn and Burnley.

I was travelling around investigating claims to ensure they were covered by the policy and if so agreeing a settlement with the claimant. The claims I was dealing with were mainly household at my junior level, the commercial and more technically complex claims being dealt with by the older man with years of experience. I was dealing with claims for fire damage which included the not so easy task of trying to establish if certain barn fires resulted from spontaneous combustion (which Mr G drummed into my head was EXCLUDED by the terms and conditions of the standard Farm Policy), damage following the bursting of a variety of water and sewerage carrying pipes and apparatus, impact damage to boundary walls and to structures, whether caused by vehicles or by livestock, storm damage both of the wind and snow varieties and burglary. Interesting work. I think that I did well, and although he wasn't one to heap praise, knew that Mr G valued my contribution to the success of his office.

After a year of driving "the rust bucket" I was told that I was to be given a different car which pleased me greatly. I was delighted when it arrived. It was a brand spanking new, bright red, Morris Mini Minor 1000. One of the first I had seen with the notchy little gear lever instead of the original three foot wand which flailed about as though it wasn't fixed to anything let alone a gear box! It was fab. I visited the local branch of Halfords and purchased a neat wooden gear lever knob, which bore the words

"Morris Mini", plus some switch extensions to "jazz-up" the dash board.

Even though the car was great I found that as the next few months ticked by I was becoming more and more unsettled at Hendersons. As I said before, the professional staff in the office comprised just little old me and Mr G. He was about 64 years of age and lived on a different planet. He reminded me of W.C Fields with a Lancashire accent. I imagined him saying,

"Hey up me likkle chickadee!" to some young and vulnerable sweetie. He was not a good boss mainly because he was tight fisted both in the passing on of knowledge and with money.

As a partner he was on a profit share of the partnership and a profit share of his Preston branch. There were terrible border disputes with Henderson's Manchester office, each branch guilty of poaching in the others territory. I recall overhearing a telephone conversation between Mr G and his counterpart, Harry Webb, at the Manchester Office,

"You know full well that anything near Blackburn is in my area so why did you send David Croft to that massive farm fire instead of sending it to me! OSBALDESTON IS IN MY PATCH. It always has been and always will be! It's bloomin' miles from Manchester. Every fool knows that! I can bet a pound to a piece of cake that if it had been a small claim you would have sent it here. I'm fed up of your tricks and I want the fee credited to my branch!"

"Calm down George you'll have a heart attack. It was a mistake. Ok? You'll get the fee credited to Preston. Don't you ever stray across our border?" replied Mr Webb.

"Hi 'ave never been so hinsulted in my life! Hi ham a man of honour!" responded Mr G. I was ear wigging from my cell of a room through the open door and thought, "You cheeky beggar! You had me going to the outskirts of Manchester last week to look at a reasonably large house fire!" Oh well. What could I do about it? ..... Absolutely nothing!

Mr G had a big belly which incorporated an ulcer. He also had full dentures top and bottom which hurt him so he would take them out and place them wherever he was at the time of taking them out. I returned them to him twice during my tenure, once from my in-tray, and once from the top of the cistern in the men's lavatory. His stomach hurt so much that when he dictated to Miss Merridew in the General Office he would press his abdomen hard against a chair back to ease the pain. He had a one ring gas stove on the floor of the general office where he cooked Ambrosia creamed rice pudding for his daily luncheon.

This all seemed normal at the time but on reflection was quite bizarre, as was his dance one Friday morning when (after apparently reluctantly watching Top Of The Pops the night before) he aped one of the performances in the General Office with Miss Merridew and me as his reluctant captive audience. "Did you see that young Lulu on the TV last night? What a daft song!" With that he set off copying Lulu's paw licking Tiger Dance singing in an out of tune Lancashire accent, "I'm a tie gurr, I'm a tie gurr, I'm a tie gurr, I'm a tie gurr r r r r r ......" I stood and watched him with mouth agape and years later saw the character David Brent from The Office TV series copying part of Mr G's dance!

The only other employee was Miss Merridew who seemed to be about 80 and who, as far as I could gather, seemed to adore Mr G. She held with disproportionate pride a tight grip on the positions of branch typist, telephonist, brewer-upper and guardian of the petty cash box keys. She kept them on a string around her neck with the keys nestling warm and damp, lost within the secret valley of her ample bosoms. Even Mr G in his capacity as a partner of the firm had the greatest difficulty in wresting them from her.

"Hi will need hay properly written voucher. It's no use looking at me like that Mr Goodall. I ham hay trained bookkeeper and will not compromise my position," she would bleat. I had a fantasy, only once mind, of the two of them being alone whilst I examined a small farm fire up the Ribble Valley. In my vivid imagination I could visualise Georgie Porgy shoving his grubby hand down the front of her Marks and Spencer (100% pure lambs-wool) twin set in search of that which would unlock the cash box.

She was both lovely, a la Hattie Jaques, and a bit of a daft old bat. She lived in the Fulwood area of Preston with her aged mother whom I guessed must have been nearly 100 years of age! I must admit, however, that she was very kind to me treating me like the son she never had. "You know what I think, James," she would say, "You have such a lovely personality, you are so good at your job and you are excellent at dealing with people that, if I were a betting lady, I would wager that one day you will be the boss of this firm." She was in tears on the day that I left Hendersons.

I had enjoyed most aspects of my Preston based job working out of a small office but, a bit like my dad who had been stuck in the office of a cotton mill had said some years before, felt I was missing out on the buzz of a larger office in a city where, hopefully, I would work with younger colleagues who would be on my wavelength.

I Did It My Way (Part II)

So here I was in the centre of Manchester driving Mr G's Morris Mini 1000 and using his petrol with every intention of leaving his employ. I parked the car on a backstreet near to King Street at about 6.15pm on that lovely summers evening. I had seen the advertisement for the job in the previously mentioned Post Magazine a couple of weeks before, had applied for the position and had been granted an interview. I knew that the relevant page from the magazine was in my jacket pocket so before leaving the car I took it out and read it once again,

"Teasdale and Harrup, Chartered Loss Adjusters, invite applications for the position of Junior Loss Adjuster at their Manchester Office. Salary negotiable. Company car provided. Applications giving details of experience and qualifications to Box 765, The Post Magazine, at the address below"

I locked the Mini and walked down a couple of back streets until I found T & H's premises, Colonial House, an impressive Victorian building comprising four floors which looked somewhat the worse for wear.

Standing on the threshold of the building I noticed a theatrical looking character smoking a Sherlock Holmes pipe. He looked as though he was in his sixties with Brylcreamed hair slicked down equal of a centre parting. He wore a crumpled woollen three piece suit in charcoal grey which drew attention to his sand coloured desert boots. I was to meet the manager of the office, Vincent Frazer, for my interview and hoped to God that this wasn't him. I had had enough of oldies!

"Jim Buchanan?" enquired the desert booted one through clenched teeth gripping onto the weighty pipe, which now sported a dangling display of saliva.

"Yes that's me.....Mr Frazer?" I nervously enquired.

"No. I'm not Vincent. I'm Albert Judd, ex Manchester Police. I work for Vince from time to time as an investigator. No. He's upstairs in the office. He just asked me to come down here and keep and eye out for you. Come along there's a lift. We're on the third floor."

We jolted our way to the third floor in the open cage lift and thus onto the landing outside Teasdale and Harrup's Manchester branch office. From within I could hear someone singing, "An...d now the end is near.... and so I face... the final curtain...."

"That's Vince!" said Albert.

As we entered the office, the singing stopped and I beheld what I can only describe as the most handsome man I had ever seen! He was the exact opposite to Mr Goodall. He had the good fortune of having olive skin, black piercing eyes, jet black hair and was about six feet tall with a toned physique. He was about thirty years of age. His immaculate dark blue two piece suit was complimented by a crisp white shirt and an understated maroon and dark blue striped silk tie. His black moccasin shoes (purchased from a shop way out of my price bracket) shone like the finest polished ebony. He was a cross between Omar Sharif and Sean Connery!

"This could be my new boss if all goes well!" I thought.

"Hi James. I'm Vince. Come in. Sit down. Let's have a chat," said Omar Connery shaking my hand with a firm manly grip. "I've read your letter and you seem to be what we're looking for. I notice that you live in Lytham. Have you any plans to move to Manchester?" he enquired. "Well, I'm planning to be married to my fiancée, Ann Crosby, and the wedding is set for about five months from now and we were thinking of moving sometime after the wedding," I explained.

"To be perfectly honest I'm not too bothered for now as we only have this one office in the North West and the claims that we are asked to deal with especially from Lloyd's Underwriters...who don't have a clue about the geography round here...can be as far away as Windermere or Llandudno. At least they pay for the petrol but there is a lot of travelling involved so you'd better bear that in mind.

Now ..... you've met Albert? Don't mind his brothel creeper shoes, he has bad feet. So would I if I'd been a bobby for forty years. He's a great bloke and since my divorce has kindly introduced me to the seedier side of Manchester's night life. We're going out tonight. He has his uses! All the club owners know him as well as the strippers, croupiers and waitresses," my new best mate, Vince, explained.

I couldn't believe the interview. It was so relaxed and friendly compared with other interviews that I had gone through in my short career. Vincent continued,

"The rest of the gang have gone home to their wives and babbies. They come out with us sometimes but don't have the staying power or freedom of me and Albert. The other guys are Dave Swinburn, who is twenty eight and is currently the baby of the group, then there's Geoff Gould, who is thirty one, the same as me.

We also have Percy who is retired and was the manager donkey's years ago. He's 72 years of age but you wouldn't think it. He's a real character and writes poems and doggerels one of which I am sure he will recite to you some day. It's entitled An Old Adjuster and it's splendid! He still looks after liability claims for an old contact of his, a leading chemicals' manufacturing company who are always having illegal discharges of noxious corrosive fumes from their two hundred foot chimney. He comes into the office every Friday to have a lunchtime drink with us, or a binder, as he calls it.

And last but not least are the girls who are great. We have Yvonne, Alma and Ruth, all young and pretty good-looking, and all keen supporters of the mini skirt, which we all agree is a good thing!" Vincent paused, took out a Dunhill cigarette from a pack of twenty, placed it between his lips like a movie star and lit it with a solid gold Dunhill lighter. He took a long draw from the glowing tipped luxury ciggy and said,

"Well I think I can offer you the job on a six month trial basis with a starting salary of one thousand pounds, which will be reviewed after the six months probationary period. There is also a company car for your sole use. I am asked by Head Office to advise you that we have a non-contributory Pension Scheme but forget that for now. What do you think?"

I was on a salary of seven hundred and fifty pounds and here was the Holy Grail of a thousand pounds that we young uns hoped for! What did I think!! I wanted to kiss his moccasins and burst into tears!

"I would love to join you and your team. Yes I really would. Can I ask what sort of car will be provided?" I ventured.

"I'm not a car man myself so long as it gets me from A to B and starts in the morning but it will most probably be a Vauxhall Viva as that's what Head Office have been sending out of late," he replied, and then, continued …. "Just one thing … bit of a rubber stamp job really … but you will have to go the Head Office in London to meet Jinks who likes to vet all the chaps who we want to employ in the provinces. Your expenses will be paid and if you would take this telephone number and ring Jinks's secretary she will arrange a mutually acceptable date and time for an appointment," he said, passing to me a sheet of paper with the phone number and the London office address.

"Can I ask, please. Who is Jinks?" I nervously enquired. "Oh, sorry! I assumed everybody in our game had heard of him. He is Jocelyn Harrup known in the City as Jinks. He is the great, great, grandson, or something like that, of the original Mr Harrup who in the seventeen hundreds joined forces with a Mr Teasdale to organize auctions on behalf of Lloyd's Underwriters for the sale of fire and water damaged goods resulting from insurance claims.

They were so successful that eventually they were contracted to actually deal with all aspects of insurance claims on behalf of the underwriters. They were in fact the original Loss Assessors which we now, of course, call Loss Adjusters. O.K?"

"O.K!" I replied, shaking hands, somewhat over enthusiastically, with my new boss.

I left the building and walked out into the warm evening air and onto the quiet post rush hour streets of central Manchester. A mass of starlings flew overhead their wings appearing to applaud my success. I was sporting a ridiculously broad grin and had the "spring of springs" in my step as I made my way back to Timoshenko.

I drove back to the coast with the car windows open and with my transistor radio blasting out. It wasn't Francis Albert Sinatra this time but Summer Holiday, Cliff Richard and The Shadows massive hit from 1963. I sang along with gusto,

"We're goin' where the sun shines brightly. We're goin' where the sea is blue. We've seen it in the movies. Now let's see if it's true ..ooooo......"

I've Been To London...

Back in Preston the following day I nervously presented my resignation to Mr G, confident, in view of what Vincent had said, that my forthcoming meeting with Jocelyn Harrup in London would be a mere formality. In any event I didn't want to delay my departure from Hendersons a second longer than necessary.

"Well we can't match their salary offer of one thousand pounds but I can perhaps increase your pay to eight hundred and fifty pounds and one day you may be offered a partnership depending how you progress," was all that he could say.

I realized just sitting in front of him and listening to his words that nothing was going to stop me joining Vincent and his colleagues. I had to work four weeks notice and had a week of holiday entitlement during that period so I phoned Mr Harrup's secretary and arranged to meet with him.

In 1969 I was a London virgin. Never been. Never felt the urge to go but I had to meet "Mister Jinks" and that meant a trip to the big city where the pavements were covered in gold or, as I was to find out, cigarette ends and litter.

So, at the age of 23, having been no further south than Buxton in Derbyshire, I was approaching Preston station in Mr G's Morris Mini Minor 1000 using his petrol once again on a day's holiday. I enjoyed the journey. Wigan, the home of Uncle Joe's Mint Balls, which my Scottish grandpa loved; Warrington Bank Quay, where the ships moor; Crewe, where I involuntarily started to hum "Oh Mister Porter what can I do? I took a ticket to Birmingham but they've landed me at Crewe," much to the annoyance of the regular travellers; Rugby, where the game comes from; Watford, where there is a gap to fill, and finally, and with butterflies in my stomach, London's famous Euston Station.

I found the steps down to the taxi rank, rank being the word because the air was filled with fumes from the taxis' exhausts. It was noisy with the diesel engine throb of so many black cabs. I joined a long queue which backed right up to the steps. The taxis looked like giant black ants in double file constantly marching slowly forward to the rhythm of their diesel engines. Finally it was my turn. Which one do I go for? There was so much hustle and bustle that I was unsure. Being a London virgin from t'North I naturally chose the wrong one!

"Here mate, you tryin' t'get me sacked? That one's before me!" shouted the Arthur Mullard of the taxi rank. Actually in my panic they had all become Arthur Mullards! "Sorry," I offered, my face saying quite clearly that it was my first time and that I was from, "Up North."

I entered the correct cab and the driver, who resembled Sid James, looked at me and without moving his lips but by raising his eyebrows cleverly asked me where I was going.

"Finsbury Circus, please," I commanded, being nowhere near as confident as I sounded.

"Finsbury bleedin' Circus! I've been sitting on me arse for arf an 'our praying for an 'Eefrow and what does the good Lord give me? Finsbury bleedin' Circus!" he ranted.

"Sorry," I whimpered apologetically. There was no further intercourse twixt me and Sid and I took the opportunity to observe the splendid churches, office buildings and shops flying by the taxi window. I was still nervous but thought that I could like London.

We arrived at our destination, I paid in silence and gave Sid a pretty good tip to cheer him up. As he drove away he lifted my spirits with a cheery shout of, "Good luck". Sid was now promoted in my mind to "Mister Kindly".

Finsbury Circus is a fantastic curved terrace of beautiful buildings. I guessed that they would have been built as homes but the majority seemed to be offices. I entered, for the first time, the grand reception area of the Head Office of Teasdale and Harrup. A very smart lady sat behind the desk. She was well dressed and sported immaculate make-up.

She would be Miss Moneypenny to my James Bond I thought.

"Can I be of assistance?" Moneypenny enquired. I can do a reasonably good Sean Connery accent but sensibly refrained.

"Yes please. I have an appointment with Mr Harrup at half past eleven," I said in a sensible voice.

"Oh, you must be Mr Buchanan from the North. How is the lovely Vincent? He is a favourite when he comes to Head Office," she purred lost in her own thoughts of my "lovely" new boss.

"He's all right. I don't know him very well. I've only met him once at my interview."

In my mind I had just promoted him to James Bond and I was now Quarrel, Bond's wide eyed sidekick in Doctor No. "If you'd care to take a seat for a minute or two please," said Miss M.

I dutifully sat down in a very comfortable chair and looked around at the photographs on the walls of fire damaged buildings, collapsed giant cranes, burnt out ships, flooded towns, exploding oil refineries and the like. Many of the photos were of international incidents as T &H had offices in most regions of the world. It made my career dealing with claims for cinder damaged hearth rugs, burst back boilers, chip pan fires and the theft of a TV or two seem a little mundane!

"Mr Buchanan," a voice awoke me from my daydreams.

"Yes?" I said with a start. It was Miss M who had

awakened me. "Mr Harrup is busy at the moment and has asked another partner Clifford Clifford to interview you. He is head of our overseas operations but has to be at Heathrow in two hours for a flight to a new serious fire claim for Lloyd's in Kuwait, so if you would quickly make your way to the second floor he will meet you."

"That's fine, thank you", I said, but I was disappointed at not meeting the big boss.

"Hi! I'm Cliff Clifford. Nice to meet you. Come on in. I don't have a lot of time," said another James Bond! Tall, well dressed, blond hair, tanned, and smoking a Rothmans King Sized, tipped cigarette. He must do well with his duty free purchases on all his travels I thought. I can't even afford a box of Swan Vestas for the odd single Hamlet cheroot that I buy! Clifford Clifford sat behind a polished wooden desk with a large map of the world on the wall behind him.

The interview went well and was more or less an informal chat. We talked a little about the insurance business, my experience so far in adjusting insurance claims and my progress in the Institute of Insurance exams (which unfortunately wasn't very progressive!). At least I was doing my best in trying to study and sit the exams for the bloomin' allotted subjects.

I found it hard to work long hours and to commit my spare time to a painful and time consuming correspondence course. I didn't reveal this to Mr

Clifford as I am not as daft as I look which my late father had always said was a blessing; he had a wicked sense of humour.

The only thing that annoyed me was when Mr Clifford asked me to point out on his massive map of the world the area that my claims work covered. I stood up, walked over to the map, found the British Isles, and indicated with a shaky finger the tiny dot that was the North West of England. I am sure he sniggered when with a theatrical sweep of his right arm across the map he said, "THIS.... IS MY AREA!"

What a plonker, was my thought, but I politely and with ever such a slight hint of sarcasm responded, "Gosh! That's interesting." The phone rang. "Yes Jinks. Mr Buchanan is still here. You can? Oh that's great. I'll tell him. Ciao," and to me, "Jinks is free now. He is coming to have a quick word."

With that the door burst open and a larger than life Dickensian figure with a wide almost wild grin stood just inside the threshold of the door. He was quite splendid. Black three piece pinstriped suit, white shirt, either a military or Old Boys' school tie, black shoes with leather tassels and a white handkerchief billowing from the breast pocket of his jacket. I took an immediate liking to him. He had a public school accent and spoke with volume but without aggression.

"Ah, Mr Buchanan. What? So sorry I couldn't see you earlier. A pal of mine from Lloyds' Underwriters who's just entrusted us with a mega fire-claim in

Kuwait asked me to pop over there for a chat and to collect the relevant paperwork. Now.... you're to join Frazer et al at the Manchester Office. What?"

"Yes, Sir," I quavered.

"Do you play golf?" the great man enquired.

"Yes, Sir," I quavered, by way of an encore.

"Perfect! You'll fit in splendidly! What? Tatty bye!"

He was gone – and I was in!!

The journey home was very pleasant and I enjoyed looking out of the train window marvelling at how much beautiful countryside there was between London and Preston.

So here was the start of another chapter in my little life. A new job, the until now only dreamed of salary of £1000, a bigger car and my wedding to Ann in a few months time.

I fell fast asleep as a result of the stress of the day, the rhythm of the train and the warmth of the carriage compartment. As I drifted off, and in the first phase of sleep, I brought to mind the sound of a girls choir singing "All In An April's Evening" so softly and gently to the rhythm of the train, something I had done before to help me to sleep. I was as content as a babe in the womb.

The train was punctual and arrived in Preston in the early evening.

I drove "my" lovely Mini back to mum's house in Lytham sad that, when I had finished working my notice at Hendersons in two weeks time, I would have to hand it back; less (of course), my gear lever knob, my switch extensions and my treasured Green Shield Stamp "clip on the window" radio aerial.

I'm not as daft as I look you know!

A New Beginning

The railway line between Blackpool Central and Preston and thereafter the rest of the world ran in front of mum's house in Ansdell, Lytham St Anne's in the glorious county of Lancashire. Sounds a bit rough until you realize that in front of the house there was a road, then a grass verge, then a British Railways fence, and then the fairway of the 8th hole of the Royal Lytham and St Anne's golf course.

It is a great hole where the teeing position is elevated to a lovely straight and flat fairway and then (bunkers allowing) a clear pitch to the raised plateau green. It is a par 4 of just over 400 yards from the competition tee the main hazard being the railway line running the length of the hole, which was naturally out- of-bounds. I could see the golfers from my bed if I was having a lie-in and spent many a late summer's evening collecting stray golf balls from the railway line and from the rough.

A charming little old chap who was a British Railways employee from the nearby Ansdell railway station had a profitable sideline in selling golf balls which he collected during his tours of the track.

I was a member of St Anne's Old Links Golf Club at the time and the "free" balls were a real bonus mainly because I lost so many myself. I had found that I was better on the snooker table in the stately wood- panelled clubhouse, nursing a pint of Tetley's, than on the golf course!

In those days the locomotives were steam powered beauties and the ones that didn't stop at Ansdell station made a splendid noise as they rushed past the house. I still have two flattened old penny coins which under cover of the dusk light I had placed on top of each other on one of the railway lines awaiting the mighty express from London via Preston to Blackpool Central. I waited until the beast had passed by and after a short search found the two coins. I couldn't believe it. The point of compression had flattened the coins creating razor sharp edges. Brilliant! And this the actions of a "mature" 23 year old trainee loss adjuster! What hope?

The day had arrived when I was to start at Teasdale and Harrup. I was up early and listened to my portable radio as I got myself ready. I still had two three piece suits of my late fathers which had been altered to fit my slimmer figure. They were pretty posh and a bit old fashioned for a junior loss adjuster, but what the heck! It was no use them going to waste.

I selected the grey check one, a white shirt and my Rochdale Grammar School Old Boy's tie, a black number with a repeated motif of a hanging fleece, which is a main feature of the town of Rochdale's coat of arms.

Mick Jagger and the other Rolling Stones were serenading me with Honky Tonk Women as I finished my ablutions and skipped downstairs.

Mum had prepared my breakfast of corn flakes, toast and home made marmalade and a cup of tea. Mum was a dab hand at marmalade making. The jar in front of me had started life as a huge can of concentrate called Ma Made to which she added tons of sugar and gallons of water. Jar collecting had been an obsession for years so we were never short of something in to which to decant the preserve.

When I had finished and with "Good luck" wishes, kisses and hugs from mum and my little sister Mary, I walked down our road around to Ansdell station singing softly, "I met a gin soaked bar-room queen in Rochdale," my version of Mick and Keith's hit song.

Ansdell station is no longer in existence although it is still a "halt". The original twin lines which used to convey the thunderous coal fired westbound and eastbound beauties have for a long time been reduced to one and now the modern diesel "bus" trains tootle back and forth invading the ears with only a polite rattle. For a minor station it used to be quite splendid, though a little frayed at the edges. An entrance lobby, with an office from which tickets were purchased, preceded covered stairs to the platforms and a waiting room, which in the winter months was warmed by a large coal fire.

It was a warm summer's day when I first boarded the substantial commuter train which would terminate at Leeds but which would make several stops, the main one for me being Salford Station, which was nearer to my new place of work than Manchester Victoria.

My fellow travellers were a revelation to me. There was one first class compartment the remainder being second class and most carriages being "Smoking." The air was soon blue with cigarette, cigar and pipe smoke. Most of the passengers were obviously regulars and worked in Manchester but chose to live on the Fylde Coast.

There were debates in progress, newspapers being studied and bridge schools in full swing. I could see into the First Class section and was captivated by the sight of a very posh looking middle aged man wearing a smart raincoat and a bowler hat which he kept on his head for the whole time. He smoked a Cuban cigar throughout the journey, as I later learned he did every working day, finishing it just before Salford Station where a chauffeur driven Jaguar limousine awaited to drive him to his office. He was a typical example of the calibre of my fellow travellers.

Vince Fraser, my new, boss had asked me to come in on the train on that first Monday to meet my colleagues and to collect my company car. He said I could add the cost to my expenses. Expenses! Hendersons never mentioned expenses when I worked for them but to be fair they had an account at Avenham Garage where I filled up the Mini with petrol. T and H didn't have such a facility so I would have to buy petrol myself and claim the money back plus any bits and pieces that I would need such as street guides and town maps.

Once the train had come to a complete standstill at Salford station I alighted and walked up Bridge Street being overtaken by the Jag carrying the bowler hatted one to his place of work; which I later established was the Head Office of an insurance company about a quarter of a mile from the station!

Within ten minutes I was at Colonial House riding to my destiny in the open-cage lift. I was nervous and hoped I was doing the right thing. I opened the dark red painted door which incorporated a frosted glass panel with the words Reception in gold lettering on it and was immediately in the general office there being no counter.

Three girls were chatting over a cup of coffee before the 9am "kick off." They looked up at this stranger on their threshold. Two of them I guessed were in their mid twenties and the third, whom I assumed was the office junior, looked about sixteen. Their hair colours were totally different. There was a long haired blond in the style of Pattie Boyd, I established that this was Yvonne, a black bob a la Audrey Hepburn, this was Alma and a natural red head with her hair cut like Twiggy who was indeed the office junior, Ruth. They were all bonny and stood up as one as I said,

"Hello. I'm James Buchanan. Mr Fraser is expecting me." I was aware that my voice was a bit shaky as I waited for a response. Pattie Boyd spoke first,

"Oh. We knew you were starting today. We've heard all about you from Vince. I'm Yvonne this is Alma and this is Ruth. How do you do?" she said as she shook my hand, "Would you like a cup of tea or a cup of coffee?"

"Coffee would be lovely, thank you very much," I replied with a smile in my voice. I sat down on one of two "visitors" seats and as there wasn't a counter felt rather exposed to the gazes of Alma and Ruth. I looked at my hands for a while when all at once Vincent Fraser came into the Reception area carrying a smart dark brown leather briefcase obviously just having arrived for work.

"Hi James," he said whilst pumping my hand with a firm handshake, "You've beaten me to it. I had a late night last night. Went to see Tony Bennett at the Broadway Club so didn't get much sleep. Yvonne can you bring two coffees to my office please?" he shouted at the doorway to the tiny room off the general office where the "brews" were made. "I'm doing it. Go through. I wont be long. Shall I bring the post in?" she shouted back in a tone of voice that implied, "You may be the boss on paper but I run this place."

It later became apparent that Vince was a good loss adjuster but not a good manager. He was happy for the girls to run the office. "Yeah. Unless Geoff or Dave are in? Give it to them to sort," and to me, "Come on James. Come through."

The office overall wasn't big. There was the Reception area combined with the General Office, the brewing-up place, a small office with one desk, a slightly bigger office with two desks and Vincent's office also with two desks. The "Gents" and "Ladies" facilities were off the communal landing, the building being multi tenanted.

"Right. Here we are! Your first day. How was your journey?" Vince enquired.

"Fine thanks. It's the first time I've come to Manchester by that commuter train. There were some interesting folk on it. They must have been doing the journey for years," I explained.

"Fine. Well, I'm out in a few minutes but we are all meeting for lunch at the Rising Sun at about twelve o'clock. I've just heard Geoff come in so I'm going to pass you on to him for the morning to show you around and to take you for your car. Ok?" he said.

"Yes, that's great. Thanks," I replied.

Yvonne brought our coffee and for a minute she and Vince exchanged tales about their respective weekend activities. She had been to Morecambe with her fiancé Ray and he had been to Old Trafford to watch his beloved Manchester United beat Spurs. Apparently Besty had been brilliantly cheeky and had laid on one goal for Bobby Charlton and scored a cracker himself. I was pleased that Vince liked United as they were my favourites too.

We finished our coffee and he introduced me to Geoff Gould before he was away to investigate some unidentified claim. I knew Geoff from my days at The Griffin and Globe's Manchester Office.

"Hello Geoff. Nice to see you again," I said as we shook hands.

A couple of years before, when I was still a clerk at The G and G, Geoff had phoned me out of the blue to introduce himself and to say that his boss (who would have been Vincent) had noticed that "The Griffin" never asked T and H to deal with any claims for them. At the time I was in a position to hand out claims but only to the loss adjusting firms that G & G already used. Geoff had said, "Can I take you to lunch and we can have a chat about it?" I had said, "Yes that would be fine thank you," knowing full well that I wasn't in a position to promise him any work... but a free lunch is a free lunch!

We dined at The Waldorf Hotel on Princess Street where on the first floor there was a posh restaurant with quality table linen, silver service and elderly waitresses in black dresses, white pinafores and white caps.

We enjoyed a three course businessman's luncheon with two pints of Boddington's bitter each. I really enjoyed it and found Geoff to be good company. He was a natural blond and a lot taller than my five foot ten at six feet two inches. He was blessed with a good strong featured face looking a bit like the golfer Brian Barnes. By coincidence Geoff was a very good golfer, playing off a handicap of six. He was 31 years of age and was married with two boys whom he obviously adored. He had been with T and H for three years. So, as I said, I already knew him.

"Hello James. Nice to see you again and thanks for the work you sent our way after our lunch. It was really appreciated," said Geoff as we shook hands.

Yes it is true! I did start putting work their way after that lunchtime meeting.

When I got back to the office replete with minestrone soup, two rolls and butter, halibut steak, tartar sauce, boiled potatoes, peas, apple pie and custard and two pints of Henry's nectar I went aided by the glow of well-being to see Frank Southern, the Chief Clerk of G & G's Claims Department. I asked him (in a confident but non-aggressive manner) if there was any reason why I should not give T and H a chance with some of our claims to see if they were any good. Mr Southern, who normally put the fear of God into me with his shouts from the back of the office of, "MISTER BUCHANAN CAN YOU COME HERE!" when he had been signing cheques which I had requisitioned, surprised me by saying,

"I don't see any reason why you should not, but keep an eye on them."

I had sent claims to Geoff and was pleased with the service which G & G received. What I hadn't realized was that since I had left the Manchester office of G & G for the Preston office and then whilst at Hendersons, the girl who replaced me had continued to use T and H and they were now receiving loads of instructions every week! I was a hero to T and H and hadn't realized. I was now given the task by Geoff to look after G & G and try to gain even more of their work in the North West. We chatted generally about this and that and after a while he said, "Let's go and get your car."

I was excited as we walked from the front door of Colonial House to a nearby garage which T and H used for service work to the cars. It was a lovely day and I was feeling pretty good. We reached our goal after about five minutes walk. A pale blue Vauxhall Viva stood on the forecourt.

"There she is. She's all yours," said a smiling Geoff.

It wasn't new, it only had two doors, it had 15,000 miles on the clock, the engine was only 1100cc, it had a dent in the passenger door and it bore registration number RJB 520F!

I must have looked disappointed and Geoff tried to explain, "You see, you WERE to get a new one but Dave kicked up a fuss, as he does, and Vince gave in to him," explained Geoff.

"What do you mean, Dave kicked up a fuss?" I enquired. Geoff explained,

"Well you've got to know Dave to understand. He's a bit of a miserable sod but he is very good at his job and works harder than anyone but he's a bit of a martyr. He has had "your" car for a year and has moaned about it for a year as he had been promised a four door 1300cc and when this came he went in a huff and has been cursing ever since.

Don't' get me wrong he's all right but he is one of life's victims. It's always the fault of someone else! You know the type. Anyway your car arrived last Friday and it was a four door, white, 1300cc, Viva and he went bananas with Vince. The result is that HE has the new Viva and YOU'VE got the old pale blue one. Ok? Are you a City fan 'cause it's their colour?"

"No. I'm a United fan, but thanks for the explanation," I replied wondering what my first meeting with Dave Swinburn would be like.

It wasn't long before I found out as it was nearly noon and Geoff led me to the Rising Sun on Queen Street for lunch. We each bought a beef and horseradish sandwich on brown bread and a half of Watney's Red Barrel. As we looked to find a vacant table, Vince and another chap walked in. Vince spoke, "Hello! How are you two rascals? Have you filled James in on everything Geoff?"

"Yeah. He now knows where the loos are so he should be ok!" laughed my pal Geoff. Vince spoke again,

"James, this is young Swinburn, who was the babbie of the team until you joined our ranks. He's been a pain in the backside with us for two years now.

Dave... meet James." Dave was smaller than me and a little on the tubby side. His hair was receding prematurely, no doubt as a result of his tense uptight attitude. He looked like a really nice guy and politely said as he firmly shook my hand,

"James, I am delighted to make your acquaintance and hope that we have a long a happy working relationship. Welcome on board."

His words both surprised and pleased me and as the months passed I realized that Dave was an asset to the office and as a perfectionist didn't suffer fools gladly, which is not a good trait, but explained his moaning demeanour. We got on well and he was very knowledgeable and helped me a lot both at work and in my studies for the Institute Exams. He was still a pain in the backside though and we all ribbed him and told him so! It was a good and happy team.

I soon met Percy Knowles, the splendid seventy two year old retired ex manager, who came in for his "binder", which comprised two half pints of bitter, every Friday and who was famous for composing the "An Old Adjuster" doggerel.

He was a grand chap of the old school, full of mischief and fun. His grandfather had been a music hall entertainer performing comic verse, comic songs and jokes. Percy told us that when on stage granddad's face was covered with black make-up and his eyes and lips were highlighted in white. He performed under the name of The Dandy Coloured Coon!

"You can always tell a woman ... You can't tell her much... You'll never find a Jew down a coal pit!" – was apparently one of his nonsensical catch-phrases. How times have changed!

One person whom Vince had forgotten to mention before was Mrs Mac, the cuddly, lovely, sixty-four-year old part-time bookkeeper who became another second mum to me. Dave had his own office as no one wanted to share with the grumbler. Vince and Geoff shared and I shared with Mrs Mac. When she wasn't in attendance the other part timers, Percy and Albert, used her desk. Neither of the pair of them were in the office much as their services were rarely required. They did however have the knack of coming into the office just before lunch!

They were great company, with a wealth of experience between them, and kept us entertained with their tales and anecdotes. Mrs Mac was very fond of me, just like Miss Merridew had been, and once said that she thought that in a few years time I would make an excellent manager and that she hoped that she would be alive to see the day.

It's another story but after many, many, years I did become the manager of the Manchester Office but by then she had long been laid to rest in her family grave at Southern Cemetery.

When we returned to the office after lunch Vince gave me some existing claim files to read and I chatted with the girls to get to know them a bit better.

In the middle of the afternoon Vince came to see me and said that we had just received a household claim for a burst pipe incident in Preston so I might as well telephone the claimants to see if they were at home and if so call on my way back to Lytham. I made the call and they were in so I agreed a convenient time for my visit, walked to the garage where RJB 520F was waiting and set forth for Preston.

Although the Viva was a bigger car to drive than the Mini it didn't feel good and sounded rough. It was also devoid of petrol so I stopped at a Shell Petrol Station on Liverpool Street in the knowledge that after spending 17s 6d on my rail ticket and 5s 0d at lunchtime I was very low on cash. As the attendant came over to the car I frantically checked my pockets and found that I only had £1 12s 0d, so I conveyed this information to the nice man and he filled the Viva's petrol tank as far as my money would allow, always ensuring that he didn't put more than my meagre amount of money would cover. He stopped the pump just in time the cost being £1 11s 8d leaving me with the not so princely sum of 4d. I asked for a receipt so that I could reclaim the sum via my expense account and with a "Tut" he duly obliged. I felt like saying, "Hang on a minute pal. I will be passing this petrol station thousands of times in the future and when I am in funds will spend loads of money with you." I didn't say it but thereafter became a regular customer and got to know the pump attendant, Jim, quite well. We regularly had those "put the world to rights" chats whilst filling up.

That first claim with T and H was with people called Bevan, a nice retired couple who had suffered the misfortune of a burst pipe in the loft of their bungalow in the Lea area of Preston. The master bedroom was pretty badly damaged by the escaping water including all the wallpaper and plaster, the skirting boards, the double bed, all of the bedding, some clothing, the dressing table and the fitted carpet.

The Bevans had already obtained estimates, all of which were very reasonable for the work involved, for both the repairs to the property and for the replacement of the damaged items of contents. I couldn't find any fault with their claim and said that I would recommend settlement in my report to the insurance company.

The truth was that they did not want to claim for certain items of damage so there was no way I could justify any reduction in the claim. I tried to persuade them to claim for those items but they would have none of it.

"We are not greedy folk Mr Buchanan and if you are prepared to recommend to the insurance company the settlement as discussed we shall be more than happy," Mr Bevan explained, his comely wife nodding enthusiastically in agreement. They were "over the moon" as they had never claimed before and their best friends had said, "You'll get nowt! It's always the same with insurance. You put good money in and you get bad money out!"

Mrs Bevan switched on the kettle and we all enjoyed a cup of tea and a digestive biscuit. I wished that all claims were as easy to deal with but knew from experience that they were not.

After saying cheerio to the Bevans I drove home to mum's arriving at the very agreeable time of 5pm. I was tired but exhilarated not imagining that I would be with the same firm for the next twenty six years!

My fiancé, Ann, was still living in Rochdale so I phoned her in the evening to tell her how my first day had been. She was delighted that everything seemed to have gone well and I confirmed that I would go straight from work on Friday evening to her parents home in Royton near Oldham where I was to spend the weekend. I was looking forward to it as I had known Ann's mum and dad Bill and Marion Crosby since we met as teenagers and had grown fond of them.

They were both very generous to we "poor young 'uns", treating us to meals with our contribution being the odd round of drinks. I knew that on Friday night after tea there would be a few bottles of beer and on Saturday lunchtime we would put on our best and visit the Summit Inn where we would eat hot pork pies and I would enjoy a Hamlet cigar and a couple of bottles of Old Tom barley wine.

We would then go back to the future in-laws home and Ann's dad and I would watch Mick McManus,

Jackie Pallo, Shirley Crabtree aka Bid Daddy, Kendo Nagasaki and Martin Ruane aka Giant Haystacks and their mates knock the hell out of each other on Kent Walton's wrestling feature within ITV's World of Sport programme. My future mum-in-law would make us a cup of tea accompanied by slices of home made buttered flat cake.

It was Ann's mum who in answer to a question from one of The Summit Inn regulars as to what I did for a job famously pronounced that I was...... "A Lost Adjuster!" A Freudian slip of some magnitude as at that time (although I never told a soul) I was struggling a bit with some of the technicalities of the job and to a degree somewhat lacking in confidence in my own ability.

On those memorable Saturdays and following the wrestling, tea and cake we would enjoy dinner in the best room and afterwards Ann and I would meet up with our pals Ian and Erica and go to one of several local pubs for a few drinks and then drive the thirteen miles to Manchester to have a curry! Don't ask me how we did it but it must be related to youth as I certainly couldn't do it now!

Let me take you back to the Summit Inn. What can I say? To little old me it was heaven on earth. Mine host was a middle aged lady named Flo Higgins who with her senior bar maid, Sally, (herself no spring chicken) ran the best pub in the area. Flo was always immaculate in appearance dressed in her finest. The lounge bar lights reflected from the polished wooden and brass fixtures and fittings and the place was always spotlessly clean.

Those Saturday lunches were great but at Christmas Flo really excelled. She spent a small fortune on festive decorations the like of which none of the regulars had seen before. The rumour was that she purchased them from London and each year they got bigger and better. Being at the "Summit" on Christmas Eve was one of the best experiences ever. Christmas songs and carols would be playing in the background and Flo would lay on free refreshments of sandwiches, pies and cake. Neither she nor Sally are with us any more but their memory, the memory of those pork pies, the cigar smoke and the strong flavour of the barley wine will never leave me.

"May your days be merry and bright and may all your Christmases be white." I love Christmas!

Back at mum's after my first day at T and H and following tea I concluded the day with a walk on the golf course. By this time all the golfers had gone home. I found two golf balls, an almost perfect Dunlop, and a Slazenger with a deep cut in it similar to the wounds which I often inflicted with my seven iron.

The following few months saw me settling into the new job and I found that I was enjoying the work and particularly the friendship that I had developed with my new colleagues. The driving was much more than I had been used to and I found that by weekend I was ready for a break.

A massive event happened in my life when on the 25th October 1969, when I had only been with T & H for a short time, the love of my life, Ann, and I were married! We were both in our twenty third year and had been "going out" since being introduced by a mutual friend when we were only fourteen years of age.

It was a splendid white wedding at a Congregational Church in Lytham known as the White Church. Family and friends helped us to enjoy a fantastic day. We held the reception at the St Ives Hotel in St Anne's and after saying our farewells drove the not very nice pale blue two door Vauxhall Viva to Stafford en route to Luton Airport. We broke the journey by staying at The Vine Inn in Stafford and the next day drove the remainder of the journey to Luton. We were in our "going away" outfits which were both formal dress and not very comfortable. New shoes were pinching feet and in my case my new three piece woollen suit was burning me up!

We arrived at the airport in good time for our flight to Majorca where we were booked for a week in the Hotel Jamaica in Magaluf. We had chatted to two other couples similarly dressed to us at the airport and found we had all been married on the same day and were all staying in Magaluf ! We made friends with them and had some great nights in the bars and clubs of the resort. We kept in touch for several years with Christmas cards and messages as to how life was treating us but eventually, as often happens, the contact was lost.

After a fab honeymoon we returned, happy and suntanned, to a semi- detached house which we had rented in Lytham. At that stage in our marriage we were certainly not in a position to buy a home of our own.

On my first day back in the office and just before lunch when all my colleagues were in the office, I gathered Vince, Geoff and Dave together and (tongue in cheek) very seriously chastised them for the content of what I knew to be their telegram (being one of the seventeen telegrams which my best man had read out at the reception).I told them in a stern voice that my new father in law was very upset when he heard my best man, Ian, read the following:-

MY DEAR JAMES...STOP...NOTHING HAS CHANGED...STOP...SEE YOU SAME TIME SAME PLACE WHEN YOU RETURN...ALL MY LOVE...RAQUEL XXX

"Was your father-in-law really upset? You're joking, aren't you?" asked Vince in a concerned voice. I paused for a while, holding on with some difficulty to a glum facial expression, and then with a great big smile shouted, "Yes I am you buggers! Most of the guests realized it was a joke straight away. Only old Aunt Annie didn't get it and later on took me to one side and said that I should have a word with that "Rachel" and tell her to leave me alone or she'll have

Aunt Annie to deal with! I'll get my own back on you lot someday. Just wait and see!"

We all burst into fits of laughter and immediately set forth in the Manchester autumnal sunshine on the short and pleasant walk to The Rising Sun where the boys raised a glass to,

"Ann and James. The Bride and Groom!"

Lawnmowers, Drambuie and Wine Gum Snakes

It is about 50 miles from Lytham to Manchester and before the construction of the M61 motorway, which links Preston and the surrounding area to Manchester, and sometime later the M55 which links the Blackpool and Fylde area to the M6 just North of Preston, I found that it was a bit of a trek to the office, especially in the winter months. I was, therefore, always pleased when Vince gave me claims to deal with nearer to home.

It had been agreed that I could still live in Lytham for the time being as it had been found by Vince and the lads in the office (all of whom lived in and around the Manchester area) that logistically my location was working out to be of some value.

We received instruction to deal with claims all over Lancashire, Cheshire, parts of Derbyshire, Cumberland and the whole of North Wales and from my base in Lytham I could deal with any claims instructed to us in the northern part of our "territory".... so long as they were not too complex or large.

We all had our limits and Vince had to be involved in any major losses as a matter of course. I was sometimes sent on "Jimmy Greens" if nobody else was free. The first time I heard the expression was when Vince called me into his office and sat me down and said, "This is a technical claim involving escape of vinegar from a massive storage tank in Trafford Park. The Underwriter wants me to deal with it but I'm tied up so can you go along and do a "Jimmy Green" for me?"

"I've heard of a Jimmy Riddle but never a Jimmy Green," I said.

"Sorry James I thought I had mentioned it before. I don't know where it came from but it's just something that has been said at T & H ever since I've worked here.

When we get a serious or large claim and we are told someone has to go straight away and there is nobody of experience available we send whoever is in to do a "Jimmy Green". You just go along, look intelligent, find out what has happened, don't say whether the claim is covered by the Policy or not, smile politely and leave. Then you tell me all about it and I take control. Ok?"

On the day that I encountered the lawnmower, Drambuie and wine gum snake I was working from home and there were no "Jimmy Greens" to be smiled politely at. I had about three household claims in the Blackpool area and thereafter it was agreed that I would dictate the reports and correspondence on my company provided, Grundig, mains- operated dictating machine.

My last appointment was in Blackpool about a mile inland of the coast in a 1930's residential area which had seen better days. I had parked up to enjoy a sandwich near "the front" watching the waves roll in from the Irish Sea. It was a sultry summer's afternoon and I felt pretty good.

The appointment was at 3.30pm so I drove my "new" old company car, the half knackered pale blue two door Vauxhall Viva, to the claimant's address. I parked, found the claim papers and glanced at the house.

It was one of a pair of ordinary semi-detached houses but my first impression was that I had never seen such a grubby looking place! The paint was peeling from the doors and windows, the dirty curtains, some half off their rails, were drawn downstairs and upstairs, and the grass and weeds were three feet in height! I doubted that anybody actually lived there.

As I walked up the path to the front door I recalled that one of the items claimed to have been stolen was a lawnmower! I thought, "What do they need a lawnmower for? They obviously don't bother to cut the grass!" I pressed the front doorbell but didn't hear it ring. I knocked on the door. No reply. I checked the file to confirm that I was at the correct address and having made sure, set off down the side of the house to the back door, stepping over miscellaneous debris including wood, glass, and poo... which I hoped was canine or at least feline.

I knocked and was surprised when the door was opened. I was face to face with a scruffy little man, bald, save for some wisps of hair over his ears, ruddy of face, slightly bent in posture and sporting a once-white shirt, stained, creased trousers held up by a length of rope, and carpet slippers.

"Mr Jones?" I enquired.

"Jess," he replied. "Jess?" I asked.

"Jess hime Nister 'ones," he said through a cleft palate.

"I'm Mr Buchanan from Loss Adjusters Teasdale and Harrup, I telephoned last Monday to make an appointment to discuss your Insurance claim. Do you remember?" I enquired.

"Jess hi wemember, Nister Uchan. Do come into the parlour," he clefted.

I actually entered a filthy kitchen my shoes sticking to the linoleum and with a smell somewhere between burnt cooking fat and sewerage offending the air. I established and confirmed that Mr Jones was the policyholder, the policy being solely in his name. I began to enquire about the theft which, according to the dog-eared claim form, was for "the theft of a lawnmower worth £200 (which was a very high figure) and £300 in cash from behind a clock on the kitchen fireplace." I couldn't see a fireplace in the kitchen. I was getting worried. I was totally unprepared for what happened next!

"My wife will deal with the craim," said Mr Jones and he never uttered another word during the following ninety minutes. He just slumped into an easy chair, which would at one time have had a pattern on it, and started to smoke a clay pipe, the content of which was probably illegal.

I stood there for a minute the only sound in the squalid room being the hiss from his pipe. All of a sudden a woman burst into the room. She looked like a wild creature, her badly dyed red hair dishevelled and back-combed, her heavy make-up old and smeared, and her eyes wide and threatening. She wore a full dark-green skirt with an elastic waistband, a red, stained blouse and a purple chiffon scarf flung around her neck in the style of Isadora Duncan. One of her dirty feet was bare and the other bore a red high heeled number. She was unsteady.

In her right hand was an opened bottle of Drambuie and in the other a plain cigarette which I guessed was a Woodbine or a Park Drive. Her overall appearance put me in mind of an over the top Bette Davis in one of her madder film roles! With an accent somewhere between mid-Atlantic and Burnley she shouted,

"Mishter Boo-canon, you are in jeopardy!" My response of, "Oh that's funny, I thought I was in Blackpool!" did nothing to lighten the mood as the tension in the room increased. She lurched and hobbled around the room, swigging Drambuie from the bottle. She stopped and held out the bottle to me saying, a little quieter this time, as though I was her best buddy, "D'yah wanna drink?"

"No thanks. Not when I'm working," was my feeble reply.

"Then have something t'eat ya miserable sod," in an accent more Burnley than mid-Atlantic.

With that she reached for a bag on the table and pulled out of it two confections in the form of wine gum snakes.

"These cost a penny each. D'ya want the red or the black?" On the word "black" she bit the head from the red snake and spat it onto the floor.

"Black, please," I ventured and continued, "Can we talk about the insurance claim, please?"

"Oh yeah. Y'see, me and Mr Jones picked up three guys in a pub in Blackpool and brought them back here for "supper"..... if yah know what I mean! In the morning they were gone and the bastards stole my brand new lawnmower and £1000 from a jar we keep on a kitchen shelf," she explained.

I was unhappy and needed a way out of this place. I had already been there about 30 minutes and had not come across anything like this before.

The lawnmower was now "brand new" and the cash amount had jumped up from the figure on the claim form and I was dealing with irrational people. I spotted on the claim form that there was no mention of the theft being reported to the police. Here was my get out ....(or so I thought)!

"Have you reported the theft to the police?" I nervously questioned. "The police? The bloody police? They're no bleedin' good to anybody!" she yelled. "I know they're not but under the terms of the policy you have to report thefts to the police," I said in a smug but rather naïve tone.

Grabbing me by the lapels she enquired as to how much money I had on me and how much my watch was worth.

"Nothing and not a lot respectively," I replied.

"Lock him in the house till the bastard pays up!" she screamed at Mr Jones who, awoken from his daydream, sprang to his feet and locked the kitchen door putting the key on the table next to the black "whole" and the red "beheaded" wine gum snakes.

"Now zen, Mishter Miserable Sod Boo-Canon, are you going to pay uppa or notta?" she demanded, temporarily transforming herself into the Bond villain Rosa Klebb.

I tried to compose myself but instead blurted out, "My job is to send a report to the insurance company with my findings and if you don't report the matter to the police I'm afraid that I can't recommend settlement of the claim," I nervously explained, as if to Auric Goldfinger as he was about to laser my crown jewels.

"Well if that's your best, then you'd better take us to the insurance company office so that they can bloody well pay up, the tight, money grabbing bastards!" she spat. I resisted this suggestion for quite sometime between spells of angry silence, pipe hissing and incoherent grumblings from "Miss Davis." I knew I shouldn't take them to the insurance company's office as my job was to act for them as their agent but I thought,

"Well at least it would get me out of this House of Horrors."

By now about 90 minutes had elapsed since I had entered this hell-hole and it was now 4.40pm. My pal David Henry was the manager of the insurance company's office in Blackpool, so I thought that, if I could make it snappy, I could get to him before 5pm when the office closed for the day. He would surely back me up, offer me some support, and confirm my conclusion?

"Ok, I'll take you, but it will not make any difference to what I have said about your claim" I replied, on the verge of tears.

"YOU just take us and I'LL sort it out Mishter Booboocannon," she slurred at me and yelled to Mr Jones, "Come on you useless dumb-brain, let's get going!"

She took the bottle of Drambuie with her and told me that she wanted some cigarettes so I was to stop at her local shop when instructed. I was soon in the fresh air and we all piled into the Vauxhall Viva. As soon as the doors were closed I was aware of the stench of old sweat, old booze and old fags and thought, "This car will need fumigating when and if I ever get home!"

We arrived at the Insurers office at 5.05pm. "Please don't be closed," I implored to the maroon painted door with the brass knocker. The door opened as I turned the door knob and although the staff had gone their merry way David was still there standing and working on some paperwork at the counter.

He looked up in surprise at the three figures facing him. We all looked similar by now because I had been sweating quite a bit and looked rather dishevelled. I explained the basic facts of the situation to him, winking frantically all the time with my face turned from the gaze of the "Claimants From Hell", hoping that he would realise that all was far from well concluding with,

"So am I correct Mr Henry in advising Mr and Mrs Jones that, unless they report the incident to the police, the claim cannot be progressed? "

"Yes, that's right Mr Buchanan,"said my saviour David, "You are perfectly correct in that if an incident of theft is not reported to the authorities then a claim of this nature can not be covered by an insurance policy as there would be a breach of a policy condition."

"Where's the safe!" screamed Bette. "Sorry?" enquired David. "Open the bloody safe and give us some money!" she ranted. David became assertive.

"I have no intention of dealing with you any further in this matter until you have reported the incident to the police."

"Nice one, Dave," I thought, delighted that he had taken control of the situation. With that she sat on the floor and dragged Mr Jones with her.

"We're not leaving here until you bloody well pay up!" she screamed.

We were in a stalemate situation. If I had been James Bond I would have pulled the winder from my Rolex Submariner, extending the wire contained within the iconic Swiss watch, and garrotted the pair of them! But I was not 007 and a mere Assistant "Lost" Adjuster.

David had had enough. "Right. That's it. I'm phoning the police," he said dialling 999 as he spoke.

"Do what you bloody well want," said Bette taking another swig from her bottle and thereafter lighting "his and hers" cigarettes. We all waited in silence but it must have been a quiet evening as within a few minutes a mature "Bobby", who by the look of him had seen it all before, appeared. David explained the position to him and George Dixon said to the "protesters", "Come on. It's no use you sitting here. Let's be having you."

Surprisingly enough they accepted his help to their feet. "She" V signed David and I with venom and "He" just looked blankly on at the scene.

They were gone and it was now 6pm and I was shattered. I thanked David and he said he would have to report the incident to his Regional Manager. He was a lot older than me but agreed that he had never come across anything like that before. I drove home to Lytham in silence, thoroughly cleaned the car inside and out and had a long hot bath.

The following day I received a gentle rocket from Vince who had had an ear bashing from Dave's Regional Manager who couldn't believe that "I" had been responsible for the "unprecedented and thoroughly unprofessional" situation which had arisen! "ME!" I thought. "God... what would anybody else have done?"

I phoned the Blackpool police the following day and they confirmed that the alleged theft had never been reported and that the pair, who were known to them, were currently in custody following a Breach of the Peace incident the night before shortly after they had left the insurance company's offices and following my nightmare claim handling experience.

I established that Mr Jones had been from a good local family but following the death of his beloved mother he had gone off the rails and the woman had got her claws into him and ran his life. She was a prostitute and was part of what the police referred to as "The Manchester Set."

I had endured a bad experience but it was pretty unique as none of my colleagues had dealt with anything like it before. As the years rolled by I found that incidents such as this were very rare.

"Did I ever tell you of the time I was locked in a house in Blackpool by a prostitute because I wouldn't pay up?"

A Hole In The Ground

"Jesus, God and fartin' nuns! How are y'FEELIN', Mishter Bukhanon?"

With those words my worst fears were made flesh as the notorious Irish insurance broker Con O'Flaherty, whose unwelcome party tricks were legendary and whom I had never met before, briefly, yet firmly, grabbed me by the balls!

I had entered the bar of The Crown on Manchester's Blackfriars Street and Vince, who was already there with Con and some other people, had just said to those assembled as I walked towards them, "Ah, Jim's here now," and to Mr O'Flaherty, "Con meet my colleague James Buchanan."

As I got over the shock Mr O'Flaherty said, "No offence son. How y'doin'. What are y'drinkin'? We're all on d'Guinness?"

"Fine thanks. Guinness would be great, thanks," I offered by way of a rather high pitched reply. Con turned to the Spanish landlady, Carmen, whom I had got to know quite well and who had a soft spot for me, to order my pint of black gold. I looked over to where Vince was standing and he winked and smiled sympathetically.

"What you doin' to Jim you silly old bugger?" Carmen threw the words at Con and slapped him round the head. She could see that I was embarrassed and I thought her reaction was splendid. "He isa ma lovely baby boy. You just leave him alone you daft old sod."

They obviously knew one another and during his efforts to fend off the blows (most of which were not very accurate) he started singing in a loud and fine Spanish accent a la tenor,

"Toreador don't spit upon the floor use the spittoon that's what it's for la la la la la la la la la la la la la la LAAAA!"

"Shut your face up. Either sing it proper or shut up you mad man," she yelled.

"Get off me you silly old tart. I was only having some fun with d'lad. Holy shite! You're worse dan d'wife," and to the assembled throng, "The drinks are on me!"

The reason that I had been asked to The Crown after work on that memorable Thursday evening was to be introduced to Mr O'Flaherty and to Dan Summers, the claims manager of the London based Constructors Accident Insurance Company Limited, and to his junior, Alan Bird, who had come up to Manchester to discuss loss adjusting services for any claims put forward by Con's very many Irish contractor and civil engineering clients.

Our firm had dealt with a few claims over the past few months but the idea was to try to reach agreement for us to deal with ALL future claims. It was a big thing for our branch and could bring in a good deal of extra work. The insurance company personnel were happy for this to go ahead it just needed Con to agree.

Whilst I had already arrived for the "meeting" Geoff and Dave were to join us which they shortly did and having met Con before and being confident in his company shouted to him as they walked into the pub, "We're shaking hands. No funny business!"

With that Con grabbed both of them around the neck in friendly wrestling head locks and said,

"Howya doin' y'auld perverts?" and to them and to the remainder of the group without taking a breath,

"Right! Let's get on with d'meetin'. Now I'm electin' meself Chairman and there will be no committee so my decision is final. Any objections? No? Good. Now den, I'm happy for T & H to deal with all d'claims involving my lovely clients but if they upset any of them I'll have their nuts in a bucket. So dats d' business sorted. Now let's get pished!"

I remember that night being a long one and thankfully Vince had asked me to stay at his flat near Bury. I had recently become the custodian of my first new car since I had joined T & H.

It was thrust upon me in that there was no discussion as to, "What sort of car would you like me dear?" No nothing like that. You just got what you got! The cars were leased from a firm in London and

I was chuffed when I handed back the knackered Vauxhall Viva to the delivery driver and took receipt of a fine four door example in turquoise with black leatherette seats of the newly released Hillman Avenger. It bore registration number XAU 352J. It was great and was a talking point in the office and with my friends as it was one of the first that any of us had seen.

Vince had arranged for the two of us to leave our cars in town at a garage which carried out service work on his posh, bright red Hillman Hunter, so I was pleased that the car would be safe. We would go to his flat at the end of the night in a taxi. We went from The Crown to The Vine, from there to The Seven Oaks, and from there the Kwok Man Chinese "eatery" for some solids!

It was an evening filled with laughter. Con was a natural comic reminding me of Frank Carson who had found fame on Granada TV's popular show The Comedians. The rest of us added our two penn'orth of jokes and anecdotes and, although I say it myself, I was pretty good at it.

Through the years these sort of affairs with clients of the company (that is: the lads who put work our way!) were not uncommon. Some would start as a lunchtime "meeting" until three o'clock chucking out time, then onto a Private Members drinking club such as The Press Club, whose committee had decided to offer membership to non-Press men in other professions in the City, and then back to one of our regular pubs for the 5.30pm opening. We were quite sporty, the drinking being mixed with the athletic games of snooker and darts!

The insurance industry was loosely based around the pubs of the city. If, for example, I had been out dealing with claims in the morning and was just getting back to the office at noonish, I knew on any particular day of the week in which pub my colleagues would be "taking luncheon."

A basic lunch would be sensible perhaps two halves of bitter and a sandwich. The normal day's lunchtime drinking would be self policed as we would more than likely be calling on claimants in the afternoon and didn't want to smell of booze.

The week after our night out with Con we received notification of our first claim for the Public Works Contractors, T.P. Connor and Sons, a long established Irish/Manchester based firm. They made their living from being sub contracted to The North West Water Authority, Norweb (the local electricity board) and to The Gas Board. I had often seen their vans at various roadsides with the lads digging up the footpath or road to solve some problem usually a leak or a damaged underground service.

It was Con who phoned the claim through to our office after first being granted permission so to do by The Constructors Accident. He wanted an urgent visit to the scene of an incident where Connor's lads had accidentally struck an underground electricity cable whilst carrying out a small repair to a gas supply pipe. It was serious!

"De shit's hit de fan, no danger!" screamed Con down the phone. "Is someone free NOW to go to Great Bridgewater Street in d'centre of Manchester?" I was the only loss adjuster in at the time hence Alma putting the call through to me.

"Hi, Con. It's Jim Buchanan here. I'm free to go and it's within walking distance of the office," I offered.

"Shite! Is Vince not der? Dis is serious!" Con's comment not boosting my slowly building confidence very much. "You'll have to do young man but take your camera so d'state of play can be on record," said Con.

"What's happened?" I ventured to ask.

"Oh! It's a bleedin' disaster. A couple of Connor's lads were digging to find a leaking gas supply pipe when they cut through d'main electricity cable from Agecroft Power Station to d'city centre. Thank shite there's a secondary emergency supply cable which kicked in immediately on impact. But Norweb are going apeshit and threatening to sue d'balls off Connor's and never use them on any of their jobs in d'future and Tommy Connor is screaming at me to do something. What does he expect me to do? I can't repair the bloody ting! Now just get down there it's at the traffic light junction with Lower Mosley Street. Connor's man is Mick O'Regan. Give me a ring when you get back."

I told the girls where I was going and with the office camera and my foolscap pad firmly in hand left the office within a couple of minutes of the call. It was under five minutes walk and I walked quickly.

As I neared the scene of the incident I witnessed a group of about ten people, most of whom seemed somewhat agitated, looking down a fenced off hole in the middle of the traffic light junction and felt the nervous semi nausea of butterflies in my stomach. The traffic was slowly moving along controlled by temporary traffic lights, which would have been set up by Connor's for the job.

I could see The Britons Protection pub, a magnificent 1800's hostelry which was near to the incident, and knew of it's near neighbour pub, Tommy Ducks, on East Street, where the ceilings were decorated with knickers affixed with nails or drawing pins and both regular haunts of employees of the insurance industry. Sadly Tommy Ducks was controversially demolished in 1993 and on the site there now stands a clinical looking Premier Inn. Thankfully The Britons Protection is still in good fettle though. I wished that I was on my way there for a pint instead of having to investigate a serious public liability claim!

I arrived at the group who watched me as I approached and said to them, "I'm from the loss adjusters acting for Connor's Public Liability Insurers. Hello. My name's James Buchanan." My split second thought was of one of my heroes facing his audience and saying, "Hello. My name's Johnny Cash." But this bunch weren't clapping.

Mick spoke first but was soon cut off by Norweb's senior man of their seven person delegation. "Tanks for coming so quick, we're in a bit of a fix."

"Bit of a fix! You're up shit creek without a paddle my friend," shouted the most senior Norweb man and to me, "Mr Buchanan, this major oil-cooled cable has been serving the city for about forty years, sitting there underground minding it's own business, when one fine day some brainless navvies rip the bloody thing in two! Thank God the JCB ... WHICH SHOULD NEVER HAVE BEEN HERE ... was well insulated or we would have a death or two on our hands!"

Mick spoke again, "Come now Mr...I don't have your name... dats a bit of an exaggeration is it not?"

"No it is not! When your firm applied to excavate here for the gas board THEY and YOU were issued with a RED notice saying that this major and very valuable cable was near this spot and that only careful HAND digging would be permitted!"

Mick climbed upon his high horse, "I take great objection to dat statement. My man Colm was carefully HAND digging when d'teeth of the JCB bucket ripped through d'armour plating of d'electric cable." (The Norweb man was now puce with rage),

"HAND DIGGING MEANS USING A SHOVEL NOT A BLEEDIN' JCB!"

Mick demounting, ever so slightly, "I take yer point, but he was operatin' d'controls by hand was he not?"

"I'll retire to a loony bin if I have to discuss this any more," and to me, "Are these halfwits insured?"

"Yes they will have the standard one million pounds worth of Public Liability cover but I've yet to establish if there is any liability," I nervously replied.

"Don't you start as well! Blood and sand! How can they not be liable?"

"Well I can only obtain the facts and report to my principals for further instruction. I would now like to interview Mr O'Regan and take some photographs," was the best I could think of in the circumstances!

"Here's my card son. Ring me ASAP and in the meantime we will try to produce an estimate as to the potential cost of the repair. I THINK a million pounds MIGHT just cover it!"

I obtained as much information as I could from Mick and took about 24 photographs, which was 18 too many according to Vince, but I was nervous of the responsibility and wanted to make sure that I had a comprehensive record of the event.

Once the meeting had broken up I walked back to the office deep in thought singing under my breath a phrase from that classic 1962 Bernard Cribbins song, Hole In The Ground.

"It's not there now the holes all flat and beneath it is the bloke in the bowler hat.......and that's that!"

A few months later after much argument over the projected cost of the repair (we engaged an expert to provide us with technical advice to ensure that the cost was reasonable) .....and with Connors trying desperately to find ways for us not to recommend settlement of the claim (no doubt with the thought in their minds of future increases in their premium)..... the claim was settled.

The final bill wasn't a million pounds but the cost of the cable and the time consuming and highly skilled jointing process amounted to several tens of thousands of pounds.

Ah! My Irish friends. I just love them.

Leading The Blind...

As time went by I found that I was dealing with the majority of the claims coming from Con's many and varied Irish contractor clients. I got to know several of the senior personnel quite well and grew very fond of them. It was always a laugh and even when I had to tell them that a particular claim wasn't covered by the terms of the policy it was always accepted in good humour. I concluded that I liked the Irish. Characters far more vibrant than the standard Englishman sprang into my life at each new claim.

There was Tom O'Dowd, the Managing Director of J.Killeen & Sons, who had a reputation for instigating and enjoying a considerable amount of entertaining of his Company's clients to "liquid lunches" to ensure that the work kept coming in. I was told by one of his employees that after one especially heavy lunchtime session he pulled up his very nice Jaguar saloon car at red traffic lights with a view to turning left into the road where his company was based.... and promptly fell fast asleep!

The breathalyser was now in full force but Tom was lucky that his secretary was walking back to the office from an errand and knocked on the car window to wake him up. He had been dead to the world despite much blaring of car horns from behind. It is reported that he was having a wonderful dream which involved kissing Ruby Murray and was peed off that he had been awoken from his fantasy!

The same Tom was the man that I had to interview to find any defence whatsoever to an allegation that when excavating near to Manchester Airport his lads had fractured a water main. There were other contractors in the area and I had been told by the site foreman that I must see his boss, Mr O'Dowd, as he held VITAL evidence that his firm had NOT caused the damage and that the claim by the Water Board should NOT be laid at Killeen's door. So I dutifully made an appointment via his secretary and arranged to meet him at his office.

"Now Mr O'Dowd, I'm here to talk about the allegations from the Water Board that your lads caused the damage to the main supply near the airport. I understand that you have evidence that it was not your firm who caused the damage," I said opening the conversation.

"Yes, Mr Buchanan I have plenty of evidence.

Firstly you can go and tell dose tossers at d'water board dat dey are a load of robbing bastards.

Turdley you can go and tell dem to shove der bloody bill up their arses and fifthly and finally if d'insurance company so much as pays dem a penny I will personally burn down der head office. Will dat do fer d' evidence? Now I'm off fer lunch so excuse me." What could I say?

"Thanks for your time I'll make a note of what you have told me," was all that I could think of.

Mr O'Dowd left the room and I went to reception to see if my pal John Milner the Company Secretary was in. He was and he was happy to see me. John usually dealt with the insurance claims and knew that I had been asked to see Mr O'Dowd for his "evidence." I told John the content of the conversation and he said that I was to forget it as it was as sure as there's a sun in the sky that Mr O'Dowd would!

It was Connor's lads who as a result of too many Christmas Eve lunchtime drinks failed to remember to fence-off a six feet by three feet by four feet deep hole in a pavement in the Piccadilly area of Manchester. They had repaired an electricity cable but were to leave the excavation open until after Christmas so that certain tests could be done to the cable by electricity board technicians. Thereafter back-filling and re-paving would be carried out in completion of the job.

In the 1970's and if it was a weekday, most building and contracting firms worked on Christmas Eve and excessive drinking at lunchtime was quite commonplace. There would be men going back to work after a heavy liquid lunch and trying to see straight to perform their duties. Some years later, and with health and safety in mind, the rules were changed and the building and associated trades very wisely finished for the Christmas and New Year break on the 23rd of December!

Unfortunately a poor soul fell down the hole in question on Boxing Day and suffered bruising and a broken ankle. Solicitors for the chap wrote to Connor's claiming that they had been negligent and seeking compensation on behalf of their client. We were asked by Insurers to investigate and if appropriate agree compensation with the victim's representative.

It had now become automatic for Vince to designate claims for Connor's to me. I arranged to meet with the site agent Terry Bones who had been in charge of Connor's skeleton staff (you couldn't make it up!) over the holiday period.

Following our discussion into the facts and circumstances we both concluded that the hole was pretty obvious and as there were some (not very well positioned) warning signs in the vicinity that we had a defence to the claim. We had to agree, however, that the barriers had been left nearby and had not been erected around the excavation as they should have been.

"Mr Buchanan," said Terry, "I know the lads should have erected the barriers but Jees d'fella went down the hole at 11am in broad daylight! What must he have been thinking about? There were "Men at Work" signs. There was a bloody great hole. There were barriers laid on the ground. There was spoil from the excavation. I mean it seems a bit daft to me."

"I take your point Terry and I will raise these matters with the claimants Solicitors when I see them tomorrow. You're right. It does seem a bit daft," I replied with confidence already mentally preparing the arguments necessary to defend the claim of negligence.

The next day I made my way to discuss the claim with Bernard Brookes of Colin & Co, Solicitors and Commissioners for Oaths at their offices on Police Street in Manchester. I had met Bernard before on other claim enquiries and although he was a lot older and much more experienced than me I knew him to be a reasonable sort of chap.

The offices were pretty grim with dark wood panelling, frosted glass windows and in need of a good clean. Following the announcement of my arrival to an elderly receptionist through a sliding window, which sported in stick-on gold letters the legend "olin & o", I was invited into a single seat waiting area with a collection of dusty old Lancashire Life county magazines, dating back between three and five years, for company.

I started to read an interesting article about the legendary trial of the so called Witches of Pendle where twenty unfortunate souls, both male and female, were tried at Lancaster Assizes in 1612 for varying degrees of witchcraft which it was alleged caused the death of about sixteen local folk. I had heard the name of one of the most notorious witches before. She was called Elizabeth Southern known locally by the scary title of "Demdike".Ten of the accused were publicly executed at Lancaster Castle!

Blimey. I thought. That's only three hundred and fifty odd years ago. How things have changed. I started to hum Which Old Witch The Wicked Old Witch as Mr Brooke's round totally bald head appeared like a disembodied warlock from around his office door.

"Come in Mr Buchanan," said the spawn of Demdike's loins, waking me from my daydream.

After the usual pleasantries which included an explanation that the sign writer was awaiting a new supply of gold capital C's and the offer and acceptance of a cup of tea I thought I would get in first,

"Now down to business!" I exploded, with a volume and with a new found confidence which even startled me,

"Connor's senior management, who naturally regret the unfortunate accident to your client, Mr Jarvis, do not deny that their representatives were a little sloppy on Christmas Eve in not erecting the safety barriers around the excavation BUT...(pause for dramatic effect)... there were signs for all to see that work had been going on and that there was a hole in the footpath which at 11am would be clearly visible," I pontificated with some conviction akin (in my mind) to the technique of a leading barrister.

I felt quite proud of my dissertation as Mr Brookes arose slowly from his chair and hooked his thumbs onto his waistcoat pockets,

"Mr Buchanan.... or can I call you James?" he said in a way which didn't require an answer. "Now let me tell YOU why WE are confident in our assertion that Connor's are guilty in negligence for causing injury and distress to our client on Boxing Day last."

There followed a prolonged professional pause much better than mine! Mr Brookes walked to his office window, looked at the scene below then turned sharply around to face me.

"Sandy, my client Mr Jarvis's four year old Yellow Labrador GUIDE DOG would ...(another wonderful pause, or should I say paws)...one would assume, have spotted the hole in the footpath and one would further assume, following his extensive training, do his very best to avoid said unwelcome opening in what should have been terra firma and thus pull his master to safety! Alas 'twas too late. And whilst Sandy stayed full square on all fours at street level, sadly Mr Jarvis was not so lucky and fell... as if he were a sack of coal (lovely pause again)... being dumped...(fantastic pause!).... into a dank and filthy cellar....being in reality the uncharted depths of Connor's excavation.

Upon the dramatic cessation of his downward trajectory he sustained a broken ankle and suffered general bruising to various parts of his anatomy!

We have a doctors report on that aspect of the matter. Now, I think I can safely say that...(another perfect pause)... I rest my case? Let's forget the tea. Do you fancy a pint? I'm parched!"

I immediately agreed to this splendid suggestion, said that I would report his evidence to my principals, shook hands and then we both left his office to walk the short distance to The Rising Sun via it's back door in Lloyd Street.

The claim wasn't discussed any further during lunch, we just enjoyed a chat about this, that and the other and each consumed a couple of pints of Wilson's bitter and a Cheese Ploughman's lunch. As I said he was much more experienced than me and I found meetings with the likes of Bernard Brookes to be very useful.

Each day I was learning more just by being with older wiser people whose knowledge and experience was invaluable to my further education.

Safe to say the claim for Mr Jarvis's injuries was paid as it is unwise to set a trap for the blind!

God Works In
Mysterious Ways.....

A few years passed by and I was learning more about the job through both experience and study. It was on the day after a severe storm in our part of the country that I met my first celebrity!

"Death is a terrible thing, – unless you are an undertaker. Storms are a terrible thing, – unless you are a loss adjuster!" said the loud voice of Tommy Farnworth, the claims chap at the insurance brokers Bentham Northern Limited.

It was lunchtime and I was sitting at a table in one of my now favourite pubs, The Rising Sun, with Dave and Geoff from the office enjoying a splendid hot roast beef and horseradish sandwich on brown bread and a half of Wilson's mild. Tommy was a friend to T and H as he had authority from Lloyd's Underwriters to instruct the loss adjuster of his choice to deal with any suitably large or complex claims which his firm's clients had made.

He valued our service and we did a good job for him, for his firm's clients and for the underwriters in that we tried to be approachable and fair as far as the insurance contract would allow. We considered ourselves to be the middle men in endeavouring to find settlement solutions equitable to all parties. I had seen some contemporaries of mine working for other firms who were a tad on the arrogant side and tended to rub people up the wrong way, which to my little mind was a totally negative approach.

Anyway getting back to Tommy. He was obviously anxious when he told me to stop drinking my beer as he had an urgent claim for me to deal with.

The date was the 15th January which was the day after a massive storm had hit the North Wales coast breaching the railway embankment (which also acted as a sea defence) near to Prestatyn, allowing the sea to flood parts of the area.

It had been reported that there was also extensive structural damage caused by the gale force winds. Tommy's firm were the brokers for Bentin's Holiday Camps who ran several sites in our region one of them being at Prestatyn. I had attended the camp before on relatively small claims and that's why Tommy was looking for me.

I had also been to the camps in Morecambe, Blackpool and Southport. Once again my home location made it efficient for me to deal with these claims which, apart from Prestatyn, were pretty local.

"So, James. Put down that beer. Get your skates on. Your off to Prestatyn ....NOW! Bentin's have been badly affected by last nights storms. It sounds really bad. Don't bother telephoning the holiday camp to make an appointment, just go! The manager, Bill Hamilton, is expecting you sometime after lunch," instructed Tommy. "Right. I'm off," I pretended to enthuse, not looking forward to the longish drive and that which what may lie ahead. It was only ten past twelve so I had plenty time to get there, view and note the damage, take some photos and see what it was all about. I did consider that this claim was a bit serious for my level but I knew that none of the others were free so I could do a Jimmy Green and wave the flag till reinforcements could be brought in, so to speak.

I popped into the office to tell the girls where I was going, grabbed my foolscap pad, the office camera and a pen, and was gone.

The journey wasn't too bad but there was still a gusty wind and occasional showers.

When I reached Queensferry my mind went back to my childhood when dad and mum took us to Criccieth for our Easter holidays.

In those days Queensferry was a bottleneck at peak traffic times and Easter was not a good time to travel. I can recall being in mile after mile of stationary traffic nudging forward a few feet every ten minutes or so.

There was a farm on the passenger side that I clearly remember as in my young, semi-comatose state I watched the farmer doing some job or other for about an hour as we slowly inched past his property.

I was most probably imagining my girls choir singing All In an April Evening as I drifted, feeling a bit car sick, in and out of sleep.

We holidayed in Criccieth for several years and we always stayed at Mrs Robert's guesthouse. She was lovely and taught me to say "Good morning, Good night, Hello and Goodbye" in Welsh making sure that I always used those words when addressing her. I can still remember the first two which sounded like, Borradah and Nosstau, respectively. Freshly cooked fish, chips and peas with bread and butter and a pot of tea followed by home made apple pie and custard was a regular and much appreciated Friday night treat in the guest house.

Sunny days were spent either on the beach, at Criccieth Castle or walking, a favourite being to Llanystumdwy where Lloyd George was born and where there was a rock by the stream where he allegedly sat and thought. I used to sit on the rock and think but being a little shallower than the great man my thoughts were on Cadwalader's ice cream and fish and chips!

I enjoyed those holidays in beautiful North Wales and the fun and games instigated by the CSSM, The Children's Seaside Sunday-School Mission, who set up camp on the beach on a daily basis.

"This little light of mine, I'm going to let it shine. Don't let Satan blow it out, I'm going to let it shine," I sang to myself as the car crossed the border into Wales.

I had visited Bentin's Prestatyn Holiday Camp before and unlike most of my calls, where I had to ask for directions or buy a local map, I knew exactly where I was going. I had also met the manager, Mr Hamilton, before and remembered him as a nice chap so, apart from the journey of over 50 miles, I was feeling pretty good. I was not prepared, however, for what I found.

As I drove down the drive through the camp gates I couldn't believe my eyes. There were roofing panels flapping about on the main buildings, chalet roofs had been ripped off and lay behind the structures in a twisted mess and the whole site was a sea of mud and debris.

The bloomin' sea had obviously paid a visit, flooded the site and gone back to where it belonged! "Vince should be dealing with this claim," I said to the dashboard,"It's massive! " But here I was representing the firm and I had better just get on with it.

I was driving my new company car a black Morris Marina coupe 1.3 (or two door as I called it spitefully), registration number WGT 624M. I had wanted a four door but didn't get it. I also didn't want a black one either which the lads teased me about saying I could do weddings at weekends and funerals during holidays. I also didn't want lime green plastic seats but Clifford Clifford was temporarily in charge of cars at the time mine was due and he didn't like requests from us on our chosen specification!

"You'll get what you get. I'm not farting about! A car's a car as far as I'm concerned," he had been overheard telling a poor unfortunate junior at London Office, which was rich coming from him, with his fabulous Citroen Safari estate car with all the trimmings! But he was a Partner so what can you say? Perhaps "Bastard! " might be appropriate.

I parked the car (that I didn't want) in the almost empty car park, and with my pad, camera and pen made my way to the Reception block. I knew the camp was closed to visitors from the end of the New Year celebrations until Easter. This was the time when the maintenance people could carry out all the outstanding jobs and perhaps some new building work could take place. I realized that the damage that I had seen so far was going to throw anything that had been planned into abeyance.

I reached the Reception building and walked up to the counter where a young worried looking woman sat.

"Hello. I'm James Buchanan from the loss adjusters representing your insurance company (no need to confuse her with the phrase Lloyd's Underwriters, she wouldn't know who insured the place).Mr Hamilton is expecting me," I said.

"Oh Mr Buchanan, I'm so glad you're here, Mr Hamilton said you would be able to sort out this mess for us," she warbled. I thought, "How can I sort this out? I'm not a builder or cleaner upper." But I actually said, "Fine. Should I wait here?"

"No. No. No! Mr Hamilton and Mr Scruggs, the maintenance manager, are on site somewhere. Just go out and have a look around and you'll soon find them. Oh Mr Buchanan, I'm so glad you're here!"

I buttoned up my overcoat, put my foolscap pad under my arm and set off to find Messrs Hamilton and Scruggs. As I walked I found myself humming or rather ding-ding-a-linging Foggy Mountain Breakdown by Earl Flatts and Lester Scruggs and wondered if Mr Scruggs, the maintenance manager, could play the banjo! I decided that I wouldn't ask him once I had found the pair of them. Yee Haa.

"Once more unto the breach dear James. Another day another claim. You'll soon be home and tucked up in a warm bed with Ann," I told myself.

It really was a disaster area. There was debris everywhere never mind the fact that every building seemed to have been visited by the sea. I noticed in the distance the breach in the railway embankment/ sea defence with the rails hanging in mid-air. "No trains for a while!" I said to myself.

After just a few minutes of searching I saw a group of people wandering about like lost souls amongst the mess. I caught up with them.

"Mr Hamilton? James Buchanan from Teasdale and Harrup acting for your insurers. We've met before when you had a claim for a break in to your office last year," I said.

"Oh yes, Mr Buchanan, I do remember you. You've found us in a sorry state today I'm afraid. I do hope you can help," said the very nice Mr Hamilton.

I had realized over the years that the best people to deal with in the negotiation of insurance claims are employees of the insured business. It is not their money that we are discussing and they are often more reasonable than the owner of the business and can understand the logic of the proposals that we would have to make and sometimes the restrictions within the insurance policy which we would have to apply. Managers, Company Secretaries, easy peasy... but not always. The worst people to deal with are householders. This is personal. It is their money. It is their home/castle and they will fight to the death to get what they think they are entitled to.

Example of a tirade following the perfectly legitimate rejection of a claim coming up:-

"YOU have the nerve to tell ME that MY claim for elephant stampede damage is not covered! I'll have you know my lad that...(and to the wife off stage)... Gladys how long have we been paying premiums for the house insurance? What? Thirty five years? (and back to me) I've been paying premiums of thousands of pounds to you lot for thirty five years and I have never claimed before ('ave I Gladys?).There have been loads of times when I could have claimed but I didn't and the first time I claim you tell me I'm not covered. Well that's it! I'm cancelling my policy and writing to my MP.

As my mate Sid, who plays darts, said the other day. Insurance is shite you put in good money and get bad money out. So what have you got to say for yourself young man?" "I want me Mammy," was what I would want to say but I could usually calm the situation down with something like:-

"I will report your comments to the insurance company and come back to you as soon as possible but, on the face of it, as you haven't got All Risks cover, the cost of repairing the damage isn't covered. Why not claim from the Circus as it could be that they were negligent in allowing Jumbo and his mates to clog dance all your garden?"

Anyway, back to Bentin's and Mr Hamilton's hope that I can help. "Well all I can do at this stage is to inspect the destruction and damage in general terms and take a few photographs. So if you would be so kind as to show me the areas of damage then I can start to make my notes.

What will happen next in view of the size of the claim is that I will have to arrange for our building surveyor, Tim Chambers, to come up from London Office to produce a Schedule of Damage so that Bentins can agree the nature and scope of the repair and then you will be able to seek competitive estimates for Mr Chambers' approval and agreement," I said, as though I knew what I was talking about.

This was a huge claim as far as I was concerned and far beyond my experience. I had dealt with zillions of household claims and claims for shopkeepers, farmers and small businesses, but this claim was going to be in the hundreds of thousands of pounds and very complex.

"Oh! I thought you would sort everything out today," replied a somewhat optimistic Mr Hamilton.

"Oh no! Consider me to be the vanguard of much more senior Teasdale and Harrup personnel Mr Hamilton. Come on, let's have a look around and you can show me the damage," I encouraged.

"Ok then. But I'm not sure that Mr Bentin will be happy that we haven't sorted something out when I phone him tonight," he reluctantly replied.

We set off with Mr Scruggs and I listed in general terms the damage suffered. Dozens of chalets were without their roofs which had been of the flat felt variety with an overhang at the front which sadly faced the prevailing wind. They had just been cast aside like a sheet of paper in front of a fan.

Within the chalets I found that all the contents, furniture, kitchenette equipment and carpets were ruined by rain and in many instances, sea water. I noted the chalet numbers with the damage relating thereto.

We then came to the main buildings including the reception and office block, the ballroom and bars, the dining hall and cafes, the shops, the nursery, the laundry and the snooker and games hall. The list went on and on. Some buildings had escaped major damage but others had serious roof damage and had been inundated by sea water.

We spent quite some time on this listing project and, being winter, it was getting dark and we were all showing signs of the stress of the day.

"Well Mr Hamilton and Mr Scruggs, thanks for your help. I have my notes and some photos so there is nothing further that I can do at this stage. I will get our surveyor to phone you tomorrow to arrange a detailed inventory of damage to enable you to obtain estimates."

We shook hands but Mr Hamilton didn't look too happy. I smiled and sighed at the same time firstly in anticipation of setting off for home and secondly because I couldn't really do much to make Mr Hamilton feel better.

"Ok Mr Buchanan. Thanks for coming so quickly, I realize that your firm must have lots of other storm damage claims to attend to after last night's storm. Have a safe journey home," said the very very nice Mr Hamilton shaking my hand once more with a firm and genuine grip.

I turned on my heels and set off to where the Black Marina with the awful coloured seats was waiting for me. I sat in the car for several minutes going through my notes and getting them in some semblance of order. Why did I not just get into the car and leave? I'll never know. I heard a voice shouting!

"Mr Buchanan! Mr Buchanan! WAIT! STOP! DON'T GO!" It was a near hysterical Mr Hamilton running at full pelt towards me and Marina. He wrenched open the door. "Oh Mr Buchanan! I'm so glad you haven't left. Mr Bentin would have killed me!" he panted.

"What's to do?" (I didn't add "chuck" to the sentence but nearly did).

"Mr Bentin has just been on the phone from a petrol station in Prestatyn. He wasn't going to come up from London today after I told him about the damage but he changed his mind during the day and will be here with his secretary and four other directors in about five minutes. He says that he is desperate to see "the insurance laddie."

A private thought came to my mind in the from of the word "Shit!" What was I going to say to the great man's questions? What frame of mind would he be in? Would he be as nice as he was on his TV adverts? God if I'd only left a few minutes earlier I would be well on my way and would pass the file to Vince the next morning with my notes. There was no doubting that this was a claim to be handled by a senior not a junior!

I became conscious of what looked like a fleet of Mercedes limousines pouring down the drive, reminiscent of a scene from the great war film The Battle of Britain when a fleet of white-wall tyred, open top tourers carrying a German General and his minions poured into a Luftwaffe base to gloat about how, "Vee are going to shrash zee RAF!" I found myself humming Ron Goodwin's evocative theme but stopped as Himler and his pals pulled up.

There were only three cars so it wasn't really a fleet but seemed so at the time. The passenger door of the lead vehicle burst open and a large man stepped out into the cold evening air.

He was obviously Alf Bentin as I had seen his likeness on the TV and in numerous newspaper and magazine advertisements. He was famous and I had never met a famous person before. He had the look of a family butcher, well washed, shiny healthy facial skin, ruddy cheeks and slicked down black hair. He was smartly dressed in a light grey three piece suit and a white shirt showing off the company tie, a maroon number with a bloomin' great golden B in the centre.

A stern looking lady stepped out from the drivers side and I later learned that this was Miss Gladys Gardner or GG.... but only if you were part of the inner circle. She was Mr B's personal assistant, secretary and Camp Commandant to the Camp Managers who, I later established, were all a bit scared of her.

Four men exited from the two other cars these being a couple of directors and the heads of group property and maintenance. Mr Hamilton almost curtseyed to Mr B and the others. I just stood there waiting for someone to say something. It was Mr B.

"Evening everybody," to the assembled and to me, "You must be the insurance laddie," and to anyone who was listening, "Get a bottle of Bells and some glasses and let's all go to the boardroom."

With that he turned on his heels and headed for the Reception and Office building. I followed clutching my pad and pen, with nothing being said.

We arrived in "the boardroom", which was a medium sized store room, but at least it housed a large table with ten chairs around it. We all sat down and the "nice" Mr Hamilton poured "nice" measures of whiskey into tumblers and passed them around as we sat down. Fortunately he had brought a large jug of water so I immediately watered mine down.

We settled in our seats with Mr B naturally being at the top with GG beside him. I looked around and thought, there are eight of them and one of me. All eyes were on me as the room went quiet. Mr B spoke.

"Now then laddie. How bad is it. How long will it take to repair the damage. How much will it cost. Will the insurance pay for everything or will we be asked to stump up something because if we are I wont be 'appy. We've been with you lot for," and to his aide, the scary GG, "How long have we been paying premiums to this lot?"

"Oh at least ten years Mister Bentin," and back to me, "Did you hear that? Ten years. So I expect you lot to foot all of the bill. Well?"

With a feeling of déjà vu it was my turn to speak. The room fell silent, all eyes were on me and when I started to speak I didn't think it was my voice. I was trying to get my brain into gear. Should I collapse to the floor and feign a fit? No come on James, say what comes out of your mouth and then get home. I impressed myself.

"Well Mr Bentin, lady and gentlemen. Mr Hamilton and Mr Scruggs have been very kind in showing me all of the damage and it is fair to say that it is extensive and will take time and a good deal of money to put the camp back in order.

My brief here today is to carry out a preliminary inspection before our surveyor from London office comes in a few days time to produce a detailed schedule of repair for your approval which can then be sent to tender to obtain the most competitive price and thereafter the work can commence," I lectured feeling pretty pleased with myself. There followed a verbal explosion !

"WHAT A LOAD OF RUBBISH! I want the repairs to start tomorrow. I can't wait for all the palaver that you are going on about. I want action. I can have men here tomorrow to start clearing up and get on with the repairs. We're closed now for a few more weeks before the season starts but my first guests The Jehovah's Witnesses, who are regulars and who are taking over the whole camp, will expect me to be open. What can I say to them if I can't accommodate them? Well? You tell me laddie!" Without any thought whatsoever I said,

"Tell them it was An Act of God."

The room fell silent! Mr Hamilton looked at his shoes. There was then an almighty roar...of laughter...thankfully... from Mr B,

"Laddie, you've made my day!" he continued laughing as did his employees, most probably for his sake and not theirs.

"You're all right laddie. Just promise something. Get your surveyor here pdq and let's all work together to get this camp back to normal. I'll get Mr Hamilton's team to start to list the damaged contents in the morning then you can come and check his list." He stood up, as did we all, and came over to me and shook my hand.

"Mr Bentin, I promise that I will ensure that there will be no delays from our side and, as you say, let's work together to get your business up and running. I'll ensure that our surveyor phones Mr Hamilton in the morning."

I left the camp rather exhausted but somewhat exhilarated and feeling proud that I had dealt with the situation satisfactorily. I wondered if Mr B might tell the tale of the cheeky "insurance laddie" to his pals or at dinner parties as the years went by. I hoped so.

Whilst Vince took control of the claim I was involved throughout including several visits to the camp to ensure that my promise was fulfilled. The camp was a week late in opening, which Mr Bentin didn't complain about, and the Jehovah's Witnesses were able to adjust their booking date without any problem.... so everyone was happy!

God does indeed work in mysterious ways.....

All's Well That Ends Well!

It was an uneventful day in the office and I was busy catching up with the dictating of reports on my allocated portable, yet mains-powered, Grundig desktop dictating machine. It was basically a posh tape recorder with a splendid carrying case with integral compartments for the transport of the machine, the hand held microphone, the patented cassettes upon which to record (which by design couldn't be used on any other competitor's machine) and the odd pen.

All the girls in the office were audio typists and had, therefore, not been required to have shorthand typing skills when employed. It was a good system which allowed us, particularly when we had a pile of dictation to do, the facility to work from home from where we could dictate our reports and other correspondence without the interruption of phone calls and chatting typists! "Hey did you see Coronation Street last night? That Len Fairclough's a rum'un! "

I was half way through dictating a sentence .... "In conclusion, therefore, we confirm that the adjustment that we have agreed with the Insured of three hundred and forty one pounds and sixty five pence net of the fifteen pound storm damage policy excess is fair and reasonable for the work involved," when Vince walked into my shared office.

"Hey! We've not had one of these for a while!" he excitedly exclaimed.

"What's that then?" I questioned.

"A claim on the Isle of Man! The papers have just arrived in the lunchtime post. This will be the first that we have received since you joined the firm. Geoff and I have been before from Manchester airport but now we have, Our Man On The Fylde, and you live near to Blackpool Airport, you are now officially given the additional prestigious title of, Our Man On The Isle Of Man!" he said with enthusiasm.

"Blimey! What type of claim is it?" I asked apprehensively.

"It's a Public Liability claim. Some contractors, Reed and Reed from the Wirral, have been building a multi-storey, multi-use block on the front at Douglas and some owners of nearby shops allege that vibration from Reed's work has caused damage to their rear yard walls.

They are apparently pretty solid stone walls some eight feet high and have been there for years and may be of historic interest. There are six complainants so it could be a biggish claim. Sounds interesting. You go and have a look and take some photographs and we'll take it from there," said a Vincent much more relaxed than I was feeling.

"I'm not a surveyor, Vince. Will it be all right me going?" I questioned nervously. "Course it will. Do a Jimmy Green and if necessary, after your preliminary inspection and depending how serious the damage is, we can appoint a local surveyor to act on our behalf. I'll just add their fee to ours. Simple!" he exuded with an air of confidence in my ability which I didn't think was warranted.

"Oh, I see. Fair enough. I'll phone Reed's and see when it's convenient for me to pay them a visit," I replied.

"Now James. Here's the most important aspect of your mission – so concentrate!" Vince was in full flow so I concentrated. "Ever since I've been with T and H I have been under strict instruction from Jinks that whenever any of us go to the Isle of Man on a claim investigation we MUST go to the kipper shop on the front at Douglas and pay them to post him a box of their world famous kippers.

Now I'll write down his address in Ascot and give you a fiver so that you can do the necessary. The next time I speak with him I'll tell him the good news and ask him to await the precious delivery. He will be thrilled and it will be a feather in your cap!

Now when you land on the island hire a mini or some other small car for the day and stick the bill for the hire charges on your Access card. You can naturally claim it back at month end through your expenses claim form.

Don't forget your driving licence and here's the fiver for Jinks's kippers. Get a receipt for the kippers and I'll send it to Jinks who will eventually reimburse me! Ok?" enquired Vince. "Ok," I replied.

Later that day I established the flight times from Blackpool International to Ronaldsway in the Isle of Man and armed with that information phoned Reed's man on the island, Peter Whalley, and agreed with him a date and time for my visit to discuss the claim and to inspect the alleged third party damage.

I asked Yvonne if she could arrange the purchase of my flight tickets and she reluctantly agreed. Yvonne was the senior typist and in her own mind only worked for the boss. Vince had told me before that as far as he was concerned the girls should work for all of us equally but, typical of Vince, he never made this clear to them which was in keeping with his unique, and by default, brilliant style of non- management! "Tell 'em nowt. Make 'em buy a programme." or "Least said; soonest mended," would not be words that Vince would utter but beautifully summed up his management technique! He was an enigma but everybody loved him.

There would be only the one claim for me to deal with on the island so as there was six hours between landing and my 5pm return I would have plenty spare time. My thoughts roamed to a nice tour of the island coupled with a quick look at the claim!

So a couple of days later I found myself at Blackpool airport mid – morning for my international loss adjusting debut. I couldn't tell you the make or model of the plane but it was small with two propellers. I had only flown on BAC 1-11's and the like before on sunshine holidays to Majorca, Minorca and the Costa Blanca, so it was a new and somewhat scary experience.

There were thirteen of us on board plus the two man crew and a pretty flight attendant named Theresa, which I thought was a great name to have in the circumstances, as one of the Patron Saints of aviators is Saint Therese of Lisieux! I could see the pilot and his mate and gained the impression that they knew what they were doing which was of great comfort to me.

The flight takes about 40 minutes and following the initial butterflies in the stomach, which invariably accompany take off, and after a few minutes of "getting used to it", I enjoyed the view from the window.

Mostly all that could be seen was vast areas of the uninviting and today quite rough Irish Sea, but occasionally I saw the odd boat bobbing along each one carrying its own wee floating community of souls bent upon their chosen activity. Without thinking I started to sing under my breath.

"Oh hear us when we cry to thee, for those in peril on the sea," and added by way of parity, "and in the air!"

I had picked up a leaflet about the island at the airport and thought it was time that I educated myself about my destination. I sat back into my seat and started to read,

"Located between England, Ireland, Scotland and Wales in the midst of the Irish Sea is the lovely Isle of Man. It is thought that the Island's name comes from that of the Celtic sea God Manannan Man Lir who is legendary for shrouding the Island in mist to protect her and her inhabitants from invaders. It is self governing and has the oldest parliament, The High Court of Tynwald (of Norse origin), in the world.

The Island is a popular holiday destination and is known the world over for hosting the annual TT (Tourist Trophy) motorcycle racing event, an international meeting dating back to 1907. The races are held on public roads which for the period of the event are closed to ordinary traffic"

"Hm!"I thought,"The TT meeting is not on at the moment, so I should have time to drive the course. Brmm Brmm!"

The leaflet went on about the water wheel at Laxey, built in 1854, being the largest in the world, and the electric tramway between Douglas and Ramsay, which also climbs from Laxey up Snaefell (2034 feet), the highest peak on the island. The reader was also strongly recommended to make a wish to the fairies when passing over the Fairy Bridge. I made a mental note so to do!

We landed in one piece at Ronaldsway and I made my way to a shop within the arrivals hall which sold newspapers, sweets and tobacco products. For the princely sum of 17 pence I acquired the Geographia Visitors Map and Guide of The Isle of Man, which in red ink incorporated the TT route!

I then followed Vincent's instructions and hired an Austin Mini 850cc, being the cheapest car available, from a local car hire firm and set off on the A5 towards Douglas (a name which my precious leaflet advised me evolved from the names of the rivers Dhoo and Glass... which enter the sea at that place).

I was looking for the A1 which would be my starting point for the TT route. "Here I am," I said to myself as I turned onto the said road to begin my version of the classic motorcycle race,

"That's it. First, into second, then third and finally smooth as silk into fourth reaching the scary speed of 35 mph! Is there no stopping this boy!"

The route was very scenic and I thoroughly enjoyed every minute. Eventually, way out into the countryside and near to Snaefell, I found a pull-in and parked "Minihirecar". Engine off. Step outside. Listen. Nothing to hear save for the song of a distant bird. Lovely!

The air was fresh and I spent some moments taking in the 360 degree panorama before setting off again and burning some more rubber. I still had plenty of time to kill before my appointment at the building site so, having completed the TT course in the record time of 42 minutes, I just let Mini follow her nose and drove here and there on the roads of this splendid Island.

A short time into my journey I saw a road sign indicating that I was approaching The Fairy Bridge. I made a wish to the fairies for health and happiness for my family and friends as I drove over the bridge and decided it was time for me to find out where the building site was located in good time for my appointment with Mr Whalley.

It was not long until I found the site which was effectively fronting onto the promenade at Douglas. It was a large three storey property which I guessed would accommodate retail units at ground floor level and apartments on floors one and two.

I parked Mini and walked to a site office at the rear of the construction site. I knocked on the door but there was no reply. I tried the door but it was locked. I looked toward the rear of the structure as a chap came out of a door into the road. "Excuse me," I shouted, "I'm looking for Mr Whalley. Do you know where he is please?"

"Yeah. He's up top with the nobs and dignitaries," he shouted back.

"Up top?" I asked quizzically. "Yeah. Go through this door and up the concrete stairs till you get to the flat roof. Be careful, there's no handrail. You'll find him up there," he very kindly advised.

"Thanks very much," I replied, and with my trusty foolscap pad, the file of papers and my black ballpoint pen, commenced my assent.

When I reached the roof I couldn't believe my eyes! There was a trestle table groaning with pies, sandwiches, crisps and cakes and a sister trestle table similarly groaning but with crates of beer and lager, whiskey, gin and vodka, bottles of wine of every colour and the odd bottle of lemonade. There was also a barrel of beer with a tube leading up to a hand pump.

There were about thirty workers gathered around and facing a chap in a suit with a chain of office around his neck who was in the throes of delivering some sort of speech. There were a number of other dignitaries standing beside him and a bonny lass in a bikini sporting a pale blue sash bearing the legend "Miss Isle of Man." One or two people turned briefly to look at me and then turned back to the speech-maker. "It is therefore my great honour, nay pleasure, to officially lay this last brick in the topping-out of this splendid new development, and may God bless this building, and all those who use and reside in her in the years to come."

The chained one made the gesture of troweling some mortar onto a brick which was duly laid and tapped into place to much applause and a little whistling. He continued, "Now I think that Mr Whalley will allow me to announce that the bar is open so please, help yourselves to the splendid refreshments which have been so kindly provided by Reed's." I noticed that at the word "bar" several of the lads rushed towards the tables and were decanting drinks before the last words of the sentence had time to drift away on the afternoon air.

A man (whom I guessed was Mr Whalley) thanked the speaker as smiles were formed and hands shaken whilst a photographer from the local newspaper did his work. Everyone then made their way toward the food and drink and Miss Isle of Man's mum placed a lightweight raincoat over her precious daughters shoulders.

There were groups of people chatting and helping themselves to drinks and food. I noticed that Mr Whalley was engaged in deep conversation with one of the dignitaries so I just kicked my heels and wandered about the roof until I saw that he was free.

My appointment had been for 2pm and it was now nearer to 3pm. Suddenly I saw that my man was alone so I rushed over before anyone else could grab him.

"Mr Whalley!" I shouted, as I ran toward him waving my foolscap pad. He stopped in his tracks as I reached him. "Hello. I'm James Buchanan from the loss adjusters Teasdale and Harrup. We had an appointment for two o'clock to discuss the claim made by the owners of neighbouring properties. Do you remember?" I asked.

"Oh! Mister Buchanan! I'm so sorry. I had forgotten that you were coming. The Topping-Out ceremony has been brought forward a day, as the member of the council, who we invited to do the honours, asked us to change the day as he has to attend an important meeting tomorrow, so we've had a bit of a rush to rearrange things. I feel awful that I forgot that you were coming. Now I'm pretty tied up for a while with the Topping-Out party, which includes a couple of my bosses, so I'll get one of the lads to look after you until I'm free." He turned on his heels and yelled, "Brian! Can you come here!"

Brian duly came, was introduced to me, the situation was explained to him and Mister Whalley went back to his guests.

"Nice to meet you, Jim," said a very pleasant Brian adding, "What's yer poison?"

"Well, I'm driving but not for a while so I'd love a pint of the draught beer please, Brian." I realised that I hadn't had anything to eat or drink since I left home and was looking forward to some food and refreshment.

"I'll go and get it, and you go and help yerself to some grub," said the very, very nice Brian. I like a man who gets me free beer!

I grabbed a large plate and piled it with pork pies, ham sandwiches, egg and cress sandwiches, tomatoes and ready salted crisps and a spoonful of English mustard. I tucked in as my foaming pint arrived. Brilliant! On the Isle of Man, enjoying pleasant weather, holding a massive plate of free food in one hand and a free pint of bitter in the other, AND getting paid for it!

Over a period of time I chatted to architects, bricklayers, joiners, plumbers, plasterers, electricians, a couple of minor dignitaries, the chap in charge of the site canteen and Miss Isle of Man's mum, Betty. I must have consumed three or four pints and plenty of food as I felt quite "content". Someone spoke to me from behind. I turned and there was Mister Whalley.

"So sorry to be so long I hope you have been looked after?" he said. I became conscious that I was slurring my speech as I responded with,

"Yesh, I have been after looked very well, shank you."

"Where are you staying tonight because as we have all had a bit to drink and time is passing by we could discuss the claim in the morning," he enquired.

"I'm not staying! I'm booked on the five o'clock flight to Blackpool International," I slurred.

"Well you'd better get your skates on! It leaves in ten minutes!" he laughingly replied.

"Bloody hell!" was all that I could think of saying.

"Hey! Don't panic! The Palace Hotel is just over there and they will have plenty rooms. Me and some of the other guys have been staying in a B&B but there's no vacancies there I'm afraid. If you like I'll come with you to book in and I can join you for dinner tonight and in the morning we can deal with the claim. What do you think?" he said.

"Well thanks for that but first of all, can I use your phone, as I'll have to phone home, phone the office, phone the car hire firm and phone the airport to book on the morning flight," I said, not feeling too happy with myself.

I completed all of the necessary telephone calls and checked into the hotel. Mr Whalley, who I now called Pete, came down to the hotel where we had a couple of drinks and enjoyed the fixed price dinner. Thankfully he paid for his meal and drinks. The old Access Card was getting a bit of a bashing!

During the meal we discussed the claim and I borrowed the waiter's pen and made notes on two paper serviettes. As far as Pete was concerned there was no damage to the rear yard walls other than ordinary wear and tear. We agreed that as I had to get off early in the morning that I would photograph the walls without Pete having to be there and then belt to the airport to drop off Mini and catch the first flight.

After dinner Pete enquired, nonchalantly, if I fancied a flutter at the hotel's casino.

"Well I've been to the Oceans Eleven Cabaret Club in Manchester with the lads from the office and during the interval twixt the comedians and the strippers have played roulette, but I don't know much about it, or any of the other casino games," I replied.

"Roulette it is then," said a confident Pete.

As we wandered through the hotel to the casino part of the building Pete started to give me a lecture on the finer points of roulette. "You can place your chip on a single number and get really good odds, but it's a long shot, you can cover two numbers with your chip, three numbers in a line, cover four at the corners......"

"Hang on a minute," I interjected, "This sounds too complicated for me. I thought you could bet on red numbers or black numbers coming up?"

"Yeah, you can but you only get odds of 1 to 1" he explained.

"So if I put a pound on red and it comes up I get my pound back plus another pound and on the roulette wheel almost half the numbers are red and half are black! Well that sounds good to me," I enthused. "It's up to you," was Pete's practical advice.

I was surprised to find a five pound note in my pocket and converted it to twenty chips at twenty five pence each. We sat at the roulette table and I played safe on red or black. Hey! I was doing well and over a short period of time I had converted my five pounds to ten pounds in chips! Pete was cursing as it was not his lucky night. He lost five pounds quite quickly so I loaned him some of my chips. The silly sod put a pound on Zero at 35 to 1 ..... AND IT CAME UP! We couldn't believe it! Chips to the value of £35 were pushed towards Pete by the non-too-happy croupier.

We were millionaires and ordered drinks, just like in the movies. I had in my pocket a tin of Tom Thumb cheroots with two of the little rascals remaining so offered one to Pete and lit both his and mine with my dark blue Ronson Comet lighter. As the smoke drifted in front of my face I said to Pete across his pile of chips,

"The name's Buchanan, James Buchanan!" We both burst into laughter and recommenced our gambling. The drinks arrived and were complimentary! Fantastic! The drinks kept coming and we kept gambling. After some time Pete said, "We've only got five quid left!"

"God! Where's it all gone?" I asked anyone who wanted to listen!

"Let'sh be bold and put the last five pounds worth of chips on RED it'sh an evens chance and I feel lucky," slurred Pete.

"NO! Let'sh think about it," I slurred back. Too late! The doubly silly sod pushed the chips onto RED as I screamed BLACK but the ball was already flying around the wheel and the croupier had said,

"No more bets, thank you, ladies and gentlemen."

The ball took a lifetime to settle down as though the croupier had, with malice aforethought, spun the wheel with extra force.

Then at last! Click, click, c l i c k, c l i c k, clickety, clickety click and the ball plopped itself, for only the second time that evening on, Zero!! We let out a joint groan.

"God, we could have won 175 shmakeroonies!" groaned Pete. Basically we were broke. We should have stopped while we were ahead. "Never again!" I swore to myself.

The evenings entertainment was done so I said goodbye to Pete and said I would be in touch about the claim in the near future. I slept well and was up early to take a quick breakfast and pay the hotel bill. I then walked to the scene of the claim and photographed the damaged wall.

I found that it was a substantial stone wall clad with "past-its-best" cement rendering. Most of the "damage" looked to me to be general weathering and problems resulting from age. There were many cracks in the render but the stonework looked sound. It stood straight as a die and showed no signs of vibration damage. I took more photographs than perhaps I should have but thought it best to be armed with a detailed visual record, mainly to save anyone having to come back for a further inspection!

Having finished my work I drove Mini back to the airport in a different frame of mind to that which I had on arrival. I felt a bit depressed but soon cheered up when the car hire chap said he would not charge me for the extra day as I had brought the car back so early.

I duly boarded the plane with only six others and was relieved that the blessed Saint Theresa was on duty to "protect us wheresoe'er we were going."

As I sat with a thickish head looking out at the Irish Sea I had a nagging thought that I had forgotten something. I only brought my coat, the foolscap pad, pen and file and I had those with me. What could it be. I suddenly remembered and much to the consternation of my fellow passengers shouted out,

"KIPPERS!"

Theresa rushed over to me.

"Are you all right, Sir?" she asked anxiously.

"Oh, yes! I'm so terribly sorry. I must have been dreaming. Sorry." The passengers nearby, realising that I most probably wasn't a lunatic after all, turned back to their newspapers and books.

"What am I going to do!" I whispered to myself, "I'm dead!"

We landed safe and sound and I made my way to the car park where Miss Marina (which sadly hadn't been stolen) was awaiting me. I drove home and phoned Vincent.

He was not happy with my overnight stay and said that he couldn't authorise my hotel bill as part of my expenses. He was grumpy but I am pleased to report that when expenses time came he relented and let me claim back my outgoings.

After asking me if I had enough dictation to keep me busy he said I should work from home for the remainder of the day. He asked about the kippers and I lied through my teeth when I said,

"Yeah. They should be on their way in the next day or two."

"Brilliant. I'll phone Jinks and tell him," said Vince. What am I going to do?

Ann came home at lunchtime from her work at a local Insurance company and, after I had explained in as much detail as I considered to be safe why I didn't come home the night before, told her about my shortcomings in the kipper department. She came up with a stroke of genius.

"Why don't you drive to Fleetwood this afternoon? There is a shop near to that large cafeteria that we went to last summer for fish and chips which sells and posts Manx kippers all over the world."

"I LOVE YOU!" I shouted, "THAT'S FANTASTIC!" adding rather sheepishly, "Can I borrow a fiver please?"

"I thought you said that Vince gave you a five pound note for Mr Harrup's kippers?" she asked with her lovely screwed up quizzical face.

"Ann. My Love. Please don't ask!" was my humble reply and, bless her, she didn't labour the point!

When she left for her office after lunch I hared up to Fleetwood, parked outside the North Euston Hotel and walked across to the Kipper Shop.

The lovely fishy people took my order for about five pounds worth of Manx kippers to be sent to Mr H at his home near Ascot. The cost including postage was four pounds and thirty five pence so I handed over Ann's fiver and I asked for a receipt.

"We don't have official receipts today as the cash register has broke and has been taken away, but I can write you one on a piece of paper if you like?" said the fish man.

"That would be great, but no need to put your address or the date on it, just write, "The Kipper Shop," and underneath just put, "To the sale of Manx Kippers and for the postage thereof £4.35p, and that will do fine."

"Certainly Sir," he responded and the job... as we say in the North.. was a good'un.

Nothing more was mentioned about my trip to the Isle of Man until about a week later when Vince came into my shared office as I was in the middle of dictating a report..... "we confirm that in compliance with the policy requirement the Insured have reported the theft to the local police who have advised us that to date there has been no progress in their enquiries."..... and said,

"Oh James. Jinks was on the phone this morning and on behalf of himself and Mrs Jinks he wishes to thank you very much for arranging for the sending of the kippers which they both truly enjoyed.

He commented that he was surprised to note that the post mark on the package was Fleetwood and I told him that I guessed that perhaps sometimes the Douglas shop asks a similar shop in Fleetwood to complete some of its orders."

"Yes I suppose they do!" was my best response continuing my dictation in the hope that he would go away...."We can, therefore, now recommend settlement of the claim in the sum of six hundred and forty three pounds and twelve pence."

"Right then. I can see that you're busy. I'll leave you to it," he said as he left the room.

I was feeling hot under the collar and knew that I was blushing but am pleased to report that that was the end of the matter! "Phew!"

A few weeks later Pete Whalley, my new gambling mate, phoned from the Island to advise that Reed's had held a meeting with the claimants and had convinced them that there was no structural damage to the walls and that Reed's, at their own expense, would carry out any cosmetic repairs so there would be no claim against the policy.

I could now close the file and submit a Final Report to Insurers stating that there had been a potential claim of several thousands of pounds but that following our investigation into the circumstances of the claim and in liaison with Reed & Reed, there would be nothing for Insurers to pay, save for our "reasonable" fees and our "not so reasonable" expenses!

All's well that ends well!

Revelations

As a group, my colleagues and I were pretty shallow in intellect. We had a bunch of General Certificate of Education "O" & "A" levels; none of us had been to university. We were Grammar School boys and had achieved sufficient GCE passes to enter the insurance industry. However, we did relish a good debate over a few pints, often with friends within the Manchester insurance community.

One such conversation between me and my colleagues from the office sticks in my mind as being particularly memorable and it involved recollections of the First World War from Percy and the dodgy subjects of Creation/Religion from Albert.

This was a major change from our usual conversations about sex, mortgages and TV programmes. We were in The Rising Sun and there was Vince (the Boss), Geoff (second in status), moaning Dave (third in status), little me, Albert Judd our super sleuth ex-bobby, and Percy our ex ex ex manager, being by far the oldest and wisest.

I had become very fond of Albert and Percy and whilst not being jealous of their ages, 67 and 75 respectively, I was envious of their "retired from business" status and their superior knowledge through experience.

"Hey Percy. When were you born?" asked Dave.

"Who me? Well it was 1897," replied a proud Percy.

"Bloody hell, that's ages ago. I don't know anybody who was born in the eighteen hundreds. Were you in the First World War," threw in an inquisitive Geoff.

"Oh aye. I was 19 when I joined the Royal Navy to train as a signalman and my first task was to join a cruiser called the Isis and we sailed from Plymouth to Halifax, Nova Scotia," recalled Percy.

"What were you doing going to Canada! The war was in Europe!" shouted an awkward Dave.

"Oh, I don't know, they wouldn't tell the likes of me! You just went where you were told to go. God it was rough. You know it took over a week and I was sick all the way," said Percy.

"Sounds as if you were on holiday!" said Dave.

"It was no bloody holiday. There were several of us signalmen and we eventually found out that we were to join convoys coming back to this country. We had some bad times and loads of merchant ships in convoys that I was with went down. I was very lucky as none of the ships I served on were hit," Percy explained.

"Oh I see," replied Dave, "It makes sense now!"

"Well if you let me finish instead of butting in you might learn something. You young lads even missed the Second World war, you've no bloody idea." Percy was in semi rant mode.

"Sorry Perse," said an insincere Dave.

"Going back to being sick for over a week and not being able to eat anything. It's really strange, but as soon as we were in sight of land I immediately felt better. I could have eaten the bloody skipper on the bridge! That's enough from me let someone else say something." Percy took a long slurp from his half of Wilsons bitter and sat back in his chair.

"Thanks Percy. I've known you for ages and never heard you talk about the war before." said Vince.

"To be honest, whilst I have some very happy memories about the times during both wars, I don't like talking about it. Much of what I witnessed I don't want to think about. You sometimes wonder if there is a God," said a sad faced Percy.

"You go to Church don't you, Jim?" asked Vincent.

"Yeah. I used to be a Sunday School teacher at the Presbyterian Church in Rochdale and still attend a Methodist Church in Lytham," I answered not sure where this line of questioning might lead.

"A Sunday School teacher! Bloody hell that's rich! What do you know about Christianity?" said Dave with his acid tongue.

"Well I've attended Church and Sunday School since I was five years of age and it's just been part of my life. I enjoy it. There is something reassuring about Church and there is peace and quiet in Church buildings. There is a mutual calmness about the folk who attend.

Two of my uncles are Ministers with The Church of Scotland, so we're a churchy sort of family.

But I'm not the type who would try to force religion down anybody's throat. You make your own mind up," I offered by way of explanation and in a tone of voice which on reflection made me feel that I was apologising for something.

"Bravo Jim! I like that. You stick up for yourself lad. Every man to his own I say," said Vince clapping his hands briefly.

There was a pause in the conversation for a moment as we supped our ale and continued to enjoy our sandwiches.

"I'm an agnostic. No one has proved to me that a God exists, but I did enjoy Sunday School. Our lot are Catholics and we went to All Souls Church in Hyde," added Geoff.

"Arseholes Church? What sort of place is that when it's at home?" said Dave.

"Don't be so crass Swinburn. Swearing doesn't become you," Vince retorted angrily.

"I'm a self confessed, third generation atheist," threw in Dave.

"What does that mean exactly? Is it not the same as an agnostic?" said the naive me.

"Well, Geoff, the agnostic, just said that no one has proved to him that a God exists and I, the atheist, don't believe in any God or divine thingy whatsoever," explained Dave impressively.

"Oh I see.... I think," was my best line in the circumstances!

At this stage the other elder statesman Albert took his dripping Sherlock Holmes pipe from between his brown teeth and asked if he could say something, "I've been around. I've fought in the Second World War, I've seen all aspects of life in my police work but I don't know if I'm a Christian, an agnostic or an atheist BUT I do have something to say about religion."

"Speak on wise sage," said Vince.

"...and onion," said cynical Dave.

"Shut up Dave!" said Vince, "Let Albert speak. Go on Albert."

"There have been so many wars and atrocities in the name of religion historically, so many incidents of...."My God is the only God so I'm going to kick the hell out of you because you don't believe in my God," that it would be better if there was no religion in the world just a mutual acceptance of each other's existence on the basis that we are all born equal and are only on this planet for such a short time.

We think that certain parts of the world contain civilised societies but the truth is that, at this stage in the evolution of the human race, we are at 1 out of 1000 in becoming a civilised worldwide society. We are Naked Apes, to quote Desmond Morris, and in the very early stages of what civilisation could become.

We can build fantastic things, but we can't peacefully inhabit the bloomin' planet! As a species we are pathetic!"

"I like that Albert. Some good food for thought there," said Vincent.

"Thanks. Just one more thing for you to ponder before we have our final pint and I shut up.

We've all seen images of what the world looks like from space, a ball, spinning around and covered with oceans, land from plains to mountains, millions of species of creatures from organisms which we can't see to the mighty elephant.

The world WAS formed or created. We know this 'cause we can see it...smell it... and feel it. It does exist.

We can speculate till the cows come home as to the origins of the world BUT, and this is point about religion, there is no reason at all why we human beings lucky enough to have been conceived and to be living on this glorious planet should not "thank," or if you like, "worship" whatever it was which did whatever it did to instigate and thus create all that the world is. If you want to call that... "whatever instigated thingy"... GOD... then fair enough. And if you believe that figures such as Jesus and Mohammed and the like are from GOD whether actually or symbolically then again, fair enough.

BUT overall we should just be thankful for our lives and enjoy what the planet has to offer and most of all be kind and considerate to others and, yes, give thanks for your life for the lives of the ones you love and for the wonders of the world in whatever way feels right for you.

In conclusion I will finish by saying that I don't believe in an "after-life" ...but I bloody well hope there is one!"

There followed a resounding round of applause from us all including moaning Dave.

"Blimey, Albert you're a dark horse! I don't know where all that came from but it is certainly food for thought. Come on lads back to the office," said Vince The Boss.

I never liked it when Vince said those words as I enjoyed these lunchtime chats and would be only too happy to stay all afternoon!

There was, however, work to be done and we weren't paid for chatting, eating and drinking!

"Have we not got time for another swift half?" enquired Albert.

"Ok then. Jim get them in. Halves for the workers and pints for our retired members, who don't have to rush back! I'll pay," said Vince.

As I drove home on that Friday night I kept thinking of Albert's dissertation and liked what he had said. It was a bit odd that he had gone on in such a way as he had never done so before.

Ann and I had a great weekend going to watch Fylde Rugby Club win at our local ground, The Woodlands, and then enjoyed a meal out with our friends, Graham and Sue, at the local Chef and

Brewer. Two pints of Henry's nectar aka Boddingtons Bitter, a prawn cocktail, fillet steak with chips, mushrooms and grilled tomato followed by Black Forest gateau with double-cream. Yummy!

I had not been in the office for long on the following Monday morning when Vince came into my room(which I shared on and off with Albert on the few times he was in) and said he had some bad news.

"Sorry to tell you Jim but Albert died yesterday morning. Well he must have died in his sleep actually as Hilda, his housekeeper, found him dead in his bed," Vince said, with tears in his eyes.

"I can't believe it Vince! Bloody hell, that's awful," I responded staring into the middle distance.

"Tell you something Jim. He had a fantastic life. Talk about burning the candle at both ends! Swales and Chesters breweries and the tobacco industry will be going bust now he's not around.

He was a connoisseur of Swales Swill and Chester's Mild, which as you may have heard is also known as Looney Soup, and Ogdens twelve-inch sweet scented flake," he paused for a moment, deep in thought, sighed and continued, "Can you get together his personal belongings please? His son, John, is coming in later to see me and I can hand them over to him. Well not much more I can say. We will all try to attend the funeral, whenever it is." He turned away from me and walked back to his office looking very upset.

The day passed with not much being said, those of us who were in the office just getting on quietly with our various tasks.

I had to leave mid afternoon to look at some fire damage to an outbuilding at a farm near Blackburn. It was up in the hills above Haslingden and when I had finished my enquiry and taken all my notes I parked the car in a lay-by overlooking the Rossendale valley and thought of Albert.

Tears began to pool in my eyes and then rolled down my cheeks more in sadness for myself and mankind than for Albert.

He would be ok. He would be sitting in some faraway sun kissed bar named The Saint Peter's Inn, quaffing a pint of Swales Swill and drawing deeply on his Sherlock Holmes pipe, giving off that wonderful aroma of Ogden's sweet scented flake tobacco which at that moment I could smell.

I don't know why, but I started singing,

"Morning has broken
Like the first morning.
Blackbird has spoken
Like the first bird."

Arson About

It was now 1975 and I had worked for T & H for six years in which time I had qualified by examination (or mental torture) as an Associate of the Chartered Insurance Institute and (more mental torture) as an Associate of The Chartered Institute of Loss Adjusters allowing me to have my business cards updated to:-

"James D. Buchanan ACII, ACILA."

Mum was proud of her wee boy's achievement and Ann was relieved that the years of mood swings during studying, and especially in exam weeks were over. The studying had been tough and the exam days even tougher. I was a nervous exam sitter and hated each examination day. I have real sympathy for those kindred exam sitters who feel like I did.

It took me a long time to qualify as you will appreciate if I confess that I sat my first CII exam in 1965!

In those days you could keep "having a go" year after year and any single subjects passed were credited toward the final target. For example there were ten subjects in the ACII course and most folk took three years to qualify. It took me ten painful years, but I was a little quicker to pass the Adjusters exams mainly because they were a bit more practical, the questions relating to the job and not to The Elements of Insurance, Commercial Practice and The Elements of English Law. It was worth the pain as gaining the qualifications was an essential step for potential promotion within the firm.

I had always been a bit jealous of Vince who being older than me had been called up for National Service.

There were a couple of reasons for my jealousy, the first being that he did his bit for Queen and Country with the RAF Military Police, which was a very lucky, cushy and privileged posting, and the second being that he was encouraged by the RAF to take the insurance exams AND given time off duty to study! He sailed through them!

People in my position had to work all day long and then try to study at night and at weekends either by self tuition or by a correspondence course both of which I tried miserably. Oh well it was now all behind me...thank God!

I considered myself to be relatively senior within the branch as by then Geoff had been promoted to the position of manager of Birmingham office and a new recruit had come in to take up my previously held position of trainee adjuster.

He was a grand chap some five years younger than me at twenty five and with experience in the claims department of one of the major national insurance companies. He was called Phil Benson and was put under my wing for training and general help and advice. We got on well and spent many a lunch hour playing the board game "Mastermind" – the one where one player hides his selection of coloured pegs from view and by process of elimination the other player has to work out the colour and position of those pegs. Great fun and a change from the pub where we used to play darts and snooker and enjoy a few drinks.

I had quite a deal of experience by now and had met and dealt with a diverse selection of people, some very nice, some unreasonable and some bloomin' awkward. There is a Lancashire expression that there's "Nowt s'queer as folk" and in my job I had come across of a fantastic cross section of humankind.

It has to be borne in mind that suffering an incident which results in an insurance claim can be one of the top stresses that life can throw at you. The top one is, I guess, death of a loved one, others being divorce and moving house. So my colleagues and I were every day dealing with people in difficult situations.

I often thought that the opposite to my job would be the man from Littlewoods' Pools welcomed with open arms when he rang the doorbell to say, "I'm delighted to advise you that your pools coupon is the only one in the country with 24 points and you have won £1,123,546!"

Often, as a result of policy conditions or under-insurance, we were giving people the news that they didn't want to hear but, as Esther Rantzen said so succinctly, "That's Life!"

Whether or not the state of the economy had anything to do with it is a matter for conjecture but there was a period when there was quite a bit of arson about.

The Strangeways area of Manchester was known for the wholesale Cash & Carry market the businesses dealing in electrical goods , fancy goods and all aspects of the fashion industry.

A local insurance broker had the monopoly of these businesses on his books and the Underwriters carrying the insurance risks used our firm to deal with any claims, and for a time there were lots! We used to come into work on a Monday morning and within minutes of the nine o'clock start we would have a call to instruct us to deal with another fire "up Bury New Road."

The broker, who I knew quite well, would want to attend the scene with me to show his clients that he was looking after them. He was a Manchester born Jewish chap of my age called Dick Edwards of Bury New Road Insurance Services.

He was a real character and we became good friends over the years. His chunky five feet nothing, bearded frame was boosted by platform soled shoes, like those worn by Noddy Holder of the pop group Slade, and his persona was boosted by a massive ego, total self confidence and a bright red Ford Thunderbird, a very rare and eye catching petrol driven beast on the Manchester scene at that time.

On one particular Monday morning he phoned with laughter in his voice and said, "Hey Jimbo! I hear you've been instructed to deal with the "unfortunate" fire at Zed Zed's Menswear Cash And Carry? Let me get there first so I can get the premium from the bastards!

They have been promising to pay for three months and we've had to fund it.

I'll say to my client that Father Christmas is on his way to pay him a lot of money so if he doesn't give me the thousand quid that he owes me immediately I'll tell him not to bother getting Rudolph out of the garage!"

Everything was a laugh to Dick. I knew that he would be crying with laughter as he told me his tactic as I arranged to meet him at his clients' premises. I then telephoned our favoured firm of Forensic Scientists to arrange for one of their highly qualified partners to meet me there. We had to try to establish the cause of the fire to ensure that the claim was fortuitous and genuine and these skills were very specialised.

I arrived at the scene with foolscap pad and camera within the hour, as did Professor David Lightfoot from Fishwick & Partners, Forensic Scientists of Wilmslow in Cheshire who, like me, had dropped everything to attend the scene of the fire as a matter of urgency.

"Dick The Broker," spoke first, "Sorry lads. Bit of misinformation I'm afraid," he said mopping tears of laughter from his cheeks.

"The bloody fire was next door at some electrical and fancy goods place but, as you can see, there's quite a bit of smoke damage in here. Sorry to have rushed you here," he apologised still in fits of laughter. I turned to Professor Lightfoot to apologise when Bob Friend of Foster & Co, an adjuster whom I knew from a rival firm, popped his head around the door.

"Sorry to bother you gents but is one of you Professor Lightfoot?" he enquired.

"Yes that's me. How can I help?" replied the professor.

"Well my firm have been instructed to deal with the major fire next door at Dians Discount Electrical Goods and we have been trying to instruct your firm to investigate the cause of the fire and your telephonist said you were already here!" said Bob. I interjected,

"Well gentlemen," I said, "This saves me some embarrassment as we at T & H don't require Fishwick's professional services as the fire didn't start in these premises! So that's great and, Professor Lightfoot, your journey wasn't wasted as Fosters' wish to avail themselves of your services and T & H wont have to pay your call-out charge!" I said, rather relieved.

Thereafter, I examined the stock of menswear, which comprised mainly formal shirts in cellophane packaging. It was clear to me that the ingress of smoke from the fire next door was minimal so I said to Mr Zed and Dick.

"It seems to me that the shirts near to the top of each stack show signs of a sooty deposit on them not much worse than domestic dust. So I have counted the exposed shirts roughly and there are about one hundred and fifty affected. So can I suggest that Mr Zed moves these shirts to the spare room upstairs, together with anything else he is worried about, then gives me a ring and I will return and agree the number of shirts and possibly other garments that are damaged."

We all agreed, shook hands and I returned to the office to dictate some reports and letters.

Two days later Dick phoned to say that Mr Zed was ready for my return visit. Dick wanted to be there so we planned a visit the following morning.

When I arrived Mr Zed looked a little coy and after the usual pleasantries led Dick and me upstairs to the once empty storeroom for us to carry out a detailed count of the damaged items so that we could agree compensation.

As he opened the door to the room where he had placed the soot damaged stock a ton of clothing in various stages of fire and water damage and general dirt fell onto us!

The room was full of damaged clothing, and not necessarily smoke damaged. Dick looked at me and burst out laughing. Mr Zed had obviously been in touch with all his mates and got them to bring round any old stock that they had from other fire, water damage or pestilence incidents in times gone by!

There were even Beatles duffle bags from the sixties and denims with fifteen inch bottoms which went out with the Ark! I stood there with my mouth wide open and Dick spoke,

"Zed, me old mate," he stood on tiptoes in his platform soles and put his arm around Mr Zed's shoulders in a fatherly way, the image of the two of them locked awkwardly together, reminding me of Eric Morecambe and Ernie Wise. "When I told you that Father Christmas was coming to pay you lots of money, I forgot to tell you that he is only kind to good little boys and girls and not to idiots who try to take advantage! Do you understand?" Mr Zed nodded his head in humble fashion and muttered, "Sorry." I took Dick to one side.

"Now there are two ways to play this. The first is that we go through the whole "fraud" thing, and the second is that he accepts my assessment of the value of his loss as a result of smoke damage based on what I saw two days ago.

So I reckon one hundred and fifty shirts at a net cost price of £2.50 each gives a value of £375 and I am prepared to recommend to Insurers a damage allowance of 40% giving a potential payment to your client of £150 and he can keep the stock and sell it at a reduced price as damaged stock. Ok?" I said in a matter of fact tone.

Dick knew me of old and whilst the Father Christmas thing was just his sense of humour didn't say anything but nodded his understanding of the situation and walked over to his now even coyer client and in an animated fashion passed on the details of my offer out of my earshot.

I could see at first that Mr Zed was unhappy but when Dick continued talking to him and made a gesture towards Mr Zed of a noose around the neck and handcuffs the claimant's resistance collapsed and the deal was struck.

I was prepared to overlook the blatant attempted exaggeration of the extent of damage as it was so naïve as to be laughable and hopefully Mr Zed and his cohorts had learned a lesson.

Regarding the business next door, where the fire originated, the Forensic Scientists investigation into the cause of the fire proved conclusively that it was as a result of arson by the proprietor.

The facts were that in the middle of the night someone had entered the premises with a key, had turned off the fire and burglar alarms with a key, had set fire to paperwork in the office with a flammable liquid (traces of which the scientists found), had forgotten to remove the liquid's container and had carefully activated the alarms and locked up before leaving.

The proprietor did not trust any of his employees and was the sole key holder. The business was financially in dire straits and substantial monies were owed to suppliers and to the Inland Revenue.

On interrogation and with so much evidence against him he confessed the crime to the Police and finished up in Strangeways Prison in sight of his burnt out business!

This information was given to me by Bob Friend, the loss adjuster from Foster & Co, whose company had been lucky enough to have been instructed by the insurers of Dians on this major fire claim. They would have been able to charge a decent fee based on the size of the claim and the complexities thereof. Our slice of the work resulting from the fire and involving Zed Zed's property was very limited, which naturally was reflected in the size of the invoice that we could submit to the Underwriters.

All in all we received our fair share of major losses and couldn't complain. Loss adjusting is a small profession and the few loss adjuster in the City were a pretty close bunch and, although we were theoretically rivals, shared information and were basically a small group of claims handling specialists working closely with each other and with the Police and Fire Brigade to deal with and settle (one way or the other) insurance claims.

After Bob had very kindly phoned me to fill me in on the conclusion of his enquiry and following the replacement of the telephone receiver on it's base

I couldn't stop myself from singing a line or two of the lyrics from the 1968 fantastic Roy Wood song recorded by his group, The Move,

"Run and get the Fire Brigade
Get the Fire Brigade
See the building start to really burn
Oooo!"

"How do you fancy three months in Cyprus?"

It was in late May 1977 when I received a telephone call from Jocelyn "Jinks" Harrup the senior partner of T and H from the Finsbury Circus offices.

As far as I could recall, whilst I had met him on a few occasions in my nearly eight years with the firm, he had never phoned me before. I was a little nervous as Alma transferred his call to my extension,

"James? Hi it's Jinks," said the plummy, public-school-honed voice.

"Good morning, Mr Harrup. How are you sir?" I replied both surprised and curious.

"I'm fine thanks. Not spoken for a while but I have a proposal for you. How do you fancy three months in Cyprus? We need someone to go there from June until September and at a partners meeting yesterday your jolly old name came up as the man most likely. What?"

"Blimey, this is a shock. I don't know what to say," I stuttered.

"Say yes, old chap!" he said with a smile in his voice, "We will pay you an extra £500 per month for the three months and if you fill in the right forms it should be tax free! D'ya see?"

"What will it involve?" I asked, thinking as I spoke that I was only on a salary of £4500 and an extra £1500 potentially tax free would be great at this stage in my married life.

"Well... loss adjusting, but in a different part of the world old thing," he replied, sounding a little exasperated, "You may recall that Vincent did a similar job for us in Kuala Lumpur a couple of years ago for eight or so weeks. Same thing really. What?"

I had mixed feelings about Vince's trip to KL. He had a ball. Best hotel, temporary membership of the Yacht Club, not much work, the claims being effectively handled by local staff with Vince as the supervising "God" figure. We had to handle all of his Manchester work though, which on top of our own workloads made it a tough few weeks. There was no suggestion of someone being brought in to fill Vince's shoes but that's how the partnership worked. I knew I had to make a snap decision one way or the other. What was there to lose?

"Ok. Can I say a provisional, yes please, but I'd like to chat to my wife Ann about it first and I'll phone you first thing in the morning, if that's all right with you?" I said.

"Super. Well done! I'm sure Mrs Buchanan will be delighted for you to have this new experience and it will be a feather in your cap for future promotion prospects. What? Ring me tomorrow. Ciao."

After he had put the phone down I sat still for a few minutes rather stunned. I mentioned it to Vince and he was reasonably happy for me but knew from past experience that I would not be replaced for the three months which would put more work on the shoulders of those remaining.

That night I discussed the proposal with Ann and, whilst she was unhappy to lose me for three months, we agreed that the extra money, especially if it was tax free, would pay off our credit card debts, leave us some spare for a few things for the house and provide a boost to our miserable Building Society Savings Account.

We had enjoyed a holiday on Crete a couple of years ago and had always fancied visiting Cyprus. Here was a chance for me to see a new place free of charge. Can't be bad we both agreed.

The following morning I spoke with Mr Harrup and confirmed that I would accept the mission.

"Splendid! Delighted! I will arrange for Cliff Clifford's secretary to phone you with the travel arrangements etc etc. What? Well done old boy. See ya."

The phone was placed on it's receiver and I sat there staring at the wall wondering what I had got myself into.

I found that my wondering was justified when within half an hour Mr Clifford's secretary (the po-faced, deadpan, Miss Hollis) phoned to ask if there was a Lebanese Embassy in Manchester.

I checked the phone book as she waited and said that I couldn't find one. "Well you'd better post your passport to me Recorded Delivery so that I can get you a visa. I need it yesterday if you know what I mean. You are flying out on the 16th of June, which only gives us 20 days. You MUST post it to me tomorrow," she commanded.

"Sorry, I'm not with you. Why do I need a visa from the Lebanese Embassy? I'm going to Cyprus."

As I said the words my mind was in overdrive. Mr Harrup had conned me. I was so naive. I was so stupid. What work could there be in Cyprus for three months? Hardly any, and certainly not enough to justify a reasonably experienced adjuster's time and effort.

"You will be flying to Cyprus certainly because that is where we have had to base our Beirut operations since the troubles flared in '75. Roger Chance and his wife, Alison, live in Nicosia but Roger flies to the Beirut office on a regular basis to see how Yussef and the secretaries are getting on.

The office closed in '75 when the sectarian violence escalated into full scale conflict. Roger and Alison had to abandon their home in the hills above Beirut as a matter of urgency. They had to shoot their beloved dog before they fled as they could not take her nor could they bear the thought of her fending for herself.

The whole thing has been shocking as you will have seen from the news over the past couple of years. Don't worry, there is now a Syrian peace-keeping force in place and things have settled down of late.

The office in Rue Verdun is once again open for business. So, basically, you will be going to Lebanon as part of your assignment."

She was quite kind in her tone of voice and must have realised that I had not been told the whole truth and nothing but the truth by Mr Harrup.

I pictured the partners meeting.

"Ok Clifford, phone James Buchanan at Manchester Office and offer him the three months in Beirut." This would be old Jinks' line.

"Hang on a minute Jinks let's think about this. We don't want to scare him off do we? You know him better than the rest of us and he will respect the fact that the senior partner has personally asked him. Roger and Alison are in Cyprus so why not just mention "Cyprus" at this stage?" This from Clifford Clifford. And finally from Mister Jinks,

"Jolly good idea. Hook him with a bun and then serve him the sour cream later. What?"

Years later I asked Mr Harrup about my suspicions and his memory of the event was that he had indeed told me all about the "Beirut" aspect of my secondment during that first phone call. I knew this was untrue, but decided not to labour the point and, with him being the senior partner, I didn't argue; although I did spot a slight twinkle in his eye as he hastily sidestepped the subject.

I had observed other examples of this type of naughty public schoolboy prank from some of the partners over the years but, by and large, they were very kind and harmless.

T and H was a "family" and it was good to be part of it. When it came to matters of commerce they were hopeless and never seemed to chase outstanding debts, especially from certain Lloyd's underwriting syndicates, who were notoriously bad payers of our fees, unless reminded...several times!

When it came to matters concerning the staff, however, they were extremely caring and supportive. "Don't worry old chap, there's enough money left in the old overdraft to pay for the odd large G and T. What?"

So I was going to Beirut! Oh well I couldn't lose face by crying-off now.

I had seen very many items on the TV news over the previous couple of years showing the fighting in Lebanon, although I must confess that, as it was all so remote from my little life, I didn't really take much notice.

I was aware, as was everyone, that there had been a bloody conflict with massive loss of life and substantial property damage.

I brought to mind an image from one news programme of a burnt out Hilton Hotel with a shattered armoured car firmly wedged in the entrance hall! So this was where I was going.

"Good luck to me," I thought!

A Character Building Experience

It was on the 15th June 1977 that Ann and I drove the now three year old Miss Morris Marina, registration number WGT 624M, mit zee awful lime green seats and laden with three months worth of my clothes, which included a Safari suit and brown suede desert boots, to London town.

I had never driven there before and it was with some trepidation that we headed south. Ann wanted to come with me on the first leg of my journey to see me off; a moment that we were not looking forward to. On the 16th day of June I was booked on Cyprus Airways flight number CY327 from Heathrow to Larnaca, Cyprus.

Miss Marina was leased by T and H from the Henley Motors Group and as the contract was due to expire, I was to deliver her to Henley House somewhere in London. I had worked out from studying my Automobile Association members handbook that it would be best to find an hotel in the North London area and as I was travelling from the NW of England I looked for a place in the NW of London.

I found the White House Hotel on Albany Street in NW1 and booked us in for the night.

On the 16th I was to call at Head Office to collect my flight ticket and Ann would say, "Take care", wave a tearful goodbye to the taxi which whisked her loved one away, and would then make her way to Euston station and catch a train back to Preston.

Following a reasonably straightforward journey we managed to find the hotel and were able to park near to the front whilst we checked-in and tried to establish the whereabouts of Henley House, which as far as I knew, could be miles away.

Following registration at the hotel I went to ask the porter for directions so that I could get rid of Miss Marina,

"You're a lucky lad and no danger. Do you see that building across the road with the ramp to the first floor?"

"Yes," I replied.

"Well that's yer 'enley 'aase!" he explained in a very enthusiastic manner.

"Oh that's great. I can't believe it! When I booked the hotel room I had absolutely no idea where Henley House was! I'll take the car there straight away," I replied with enthusiasm. That was a stroke of immense good luck and I hoped it would be a good omen for the next three months.

After spending a restless night being serenaded by emergency services' sirens, a general hubbub, hotel doors slamming and the usual hotel droning sound, we enjoyed a delightful English breakfast and then taxied to Finsbury Circus.

Both Cliff Clifford and Mr Harrup came down to reception to meet us and my ticket was duly handed over.

The receptionist asked if I had managed to deliver Marina to Henley's and I confirmed that I had done so. At this juncture Cliff Clifford jumped in.

"Oh yes, James, that reminds me. When you get back in September your new car will be here for you to pick up."

"Oh that's good. Do you know what it will be?" I enquired.

"Yes it will be a Ford Capri. Before you ask... I don't know which model nor what colour it will be, because I have no idea!"

With that we all laughed and said our goodbyes and Ann and I left to meet her cousin Barry, who worked in London, and who was to take her for lunch and make sure she got to Euston safely. We met up with Barry and then it was "farewell time" and following a few tears I hailed a cab for Heathrow.

So I was now on my own at the start of my adventure and upon my return I would be the custodian of a lovely Ford Capri. This was a much better car than the Marina and I wondered if my acceptance of the Beirut secondment had got something to do with it? This was something to look forward to during my three months away.

The taxi driver, who looked like Bernard Bresslaw of Carry On and Mad Passionate Love fame, had asked which terminal I wanted. We chatted and he asked if I was going somewhere nice. I said "Beirut." His response of "Blimey Charlie!" did nothing for my confidence!

The instructions from the firm's travel agents said Terminal 2 so that's where me and Bernard went. When I tried to find where to check-in I thought that I must have the wrong day as I couldn't find my flight anywhere. I went to the information desk and was told I was at the wrong terminal and should have been at Terminal 1. "Bloomin' travel agents," I cursed to myself. This really got me in a state as time was pressing.

There was a link bus service which I duly caught and relieved, arrived in plenty time for check-in. The plane was boarded and then came the announcement.

I was aware that The Commonwealth Conference had been held in London but it was a surprise to all when the captain told us that we were making an unscheduled stop at Athens to drop off a VIP. The chap beside me said that he thought it would be Archbishop Makarios, the President of Cyprus, and he was correct, as when we landed at our unscheduled stop I saw him on the tarmac being greeted by officials. "Crikey nothing seems to be normal on this trip," I thought.

I was surprised to hear some weeks later that the Archbishop had died on the 3rd of August 1977 just 13 days before the death of one of my heroes, Elvis, who sadly passed away on the 16th at the young age of 42. I heard the news of the death of Elvis whilst lying on my hotel bed in Beirut late one afternoon listening to a local Lebanese radio station.

I remember wondering why they were playing non-stop Elvis. It wasn't until a break in the music that the announcer explained that the wall to wall Elvis was a tribute to the King, as he had passed away. Like all other fans I was shocked.

However, I am getting ahead of myself.

The flight was good and I chatted with the pleasant chap beside me about this and that and was jealous that his visit to Cyprus was to holiday with Cypriot friends. He told me that they had owned a beautiful house and business in Famagusta in the northern part of the island which they had been forced to abandon in 1974.

The reason they had to leave was that Turkish troops, without any warning, invaded Cyprus resulting in the northern part of the island, including land and property, being grabbed by them.

His pals apparently lost everything and had to start out again in the south. He told me that since 1974, approximately 40% of the island had been under illegal Turkish occupation.

"Unbelievable," I said, "Let's hope that the invaders soon go back to Turkey so that your friends can go back home." He grunted in unconvinced agreement, the conversation concluded and I drifted into a deep sleep.

I was awoken sometime later by an announcement from one of the cabin crew that we were about to land at Larnaka airport.

Horticulture, Hilton
and Her Majesty

I decanted myself from the plane together with my fellow travellers and made my way to the Arrivals Hall.

It was not a splendid place by any means and had a rather makeshift, practical feel to it. The main airport at Nicosia had been captured by the Turkish forces during their invasion and Larnaca, which had been a small regional airport, had been adopted as the airport now serving the Greek Cypriot south of the island.

I didn't need a visa for Cyprus but did for Beirut and my passport incorporated a visa from The Embassy of Lebanon emblazoned with an image of the Cedar Tree, the symbol of that ravaged country.

The very pleasant gentleman at Cyprus immigration control asked if I was visiting on business or pleasure and when I declared "business" my passport was marked that I could stay for no longer than three months. A page of my passport received the appropriate rubber stamp and the official wrote in red ink within the stamped image the date "16th September 1977", the sight of which caused a sudden ache in the pit of my stomach at the thought of what the events of the next twelve weeks might throw at me.

I could see all those waiting for loved ones and friends from where I was queuing on the immigration control side of a flimsy barrier which was the rear of an open stand displaying newspapers and confectionery.

We could almost touch those who were waiting to meet us as they were only a few feet away.

I soon picked out who I guessed to be my new temporary boss, Roger Chance, and found that I was correct in my assumption as I entered the arrivals lobby. Did this firm only recruit James Bond types for their overseas operations? He was about six feet and three inches tall with a deep tan, black hair going grey at the temples and a weathered, lived-in-face, his overall look reminding me of James Coburn.

He wore a duck egg blue, short sleeved shirt, which to my mind must have been sea island cotton, and dark blue slacks with a shiny leather belt. His feet were clad in dusty black leather desert boots. On his thick, tanned left wrist he sported a stainless steel Rolex Submariner watch with a black crocodile strap, something that had been on my wish list since the release of the first Bond film, Dr No, in 1962.

He had also assumed that I was the chap that he was waiting for as he came right over to me and with a firm handshake said,

"James Buchanan I presume? I'm Roger Chance. Welcome to a very hot Cyprus."

He was right. It was bloomin' hot as there was no air conditioning in the airport, just the odd lazy, creaking ceiling fan moving the hot air around.

It was about 10.45 pm local time. Roger explained that it had been in the mid 90's Fahrenheit all day and that buildings, particularly those constructed from concrete, effectively acted as storage heaters during the day and discharged heat from their fabric all night long ready for the next day's heat-up!

"I have at last just managed to buy an air conditioning unit for the bungalow that the firm are renting in Nicosia and a neighbour installed it in the master bedroom today. God it's been stifling for the past two weeks. Alison hasn't been able to sleep. There's hardly been a cloud in the sky.

Anyway we'll get your case, then it's about 32 miles, which should take 45 minutes, over the hills to Kalypsos Street where the bungalow is," he explained in a pleasant yet authoritative tone of voice.

When my baggage had been collected we walked out into the hot evening air to a neat, two door, Renault 5 bearing registration number HZ 875. She was bright yellow, which I thought was a great colour for a car on this sunny Mediterranean island. I immediately christened her Heinz but didn't tell Roger!

So off we set across the hills of this enchanting yet divided island. An island that over the years Ann and I would grow to love.

We didn't arrive at the company bungalow until midnight and straight away Roger showed me to my room and to where the bathroom was. We bade each other goodnight and he went off to join his wife.

I was soon in my bed feeling a bit shattered both physically and emotionally. There was light coming through the thin curtains and as I lay on my back I saw a large creepy crawly on the ceiling directly over my face!

Just like Bond in Dr No when he smashed the tarantula to smithereens, I shot out of bed, bashed it from the ceiling to the floor with my trousers, chased it round the room and then beat it to death with one of my shoes.

A voice came from the other room.

"Everything all right James?"

I shouted back words which I couldn't believe I said, "Roger....Roger! All's well thank you!"

I was soon in a deep sleep. The next thing I became aware of was a knock on the door and Roger's voice,

"You staying there all day James? It's nearly ten o'clock."

"Sorry Roger. Must have overslept. Be with you shortly," I replied through a yawn. I had slept very well and though groggy knew that the sleep had done me good. I was quickly up, showered and dressed in slacks and a thin short sleeved shirt. I made my way to the sound of voices coming from the kitchen.

"Ah, there you are James! Let me introduce you to Alison, my long suffering wife," said Roger.

"Hello I'm very pleased to meet you, and thanks for having me," I said to Alison, who was about my height and who was blessed with that pale skinned, blond look of the English Rose. She looked as though she had had enough of her international loss adjusting husband's lifestyle in the heat of the Middle East. She didn't look too happy. I assessed that she was about 45 years of age and was aware that her three daughters were all in the UK at boarding school. She probably missed them terribly. She sighed her reply as we shook damp hands. It was very hot.

"Nice to meet you James. I hope you are feeling strong?"

Strong? What's that all about! I thought. Roger explained.

"Ah yes. We are developing the garden and have a couple of tons of top soil arriving shortly. I thought you and I could shovel it into the garden and then we can take Alison to the garden centre for her to buy some plants and shrubs."

What was he talking about? I had left loads of outstanding work on my desk in Manchester with the ambitious hope that Vincent would pass it around the office to the others to finish off my claims. I knew he would struggle persuading my colleagues as they were all very busy with new work pouring in daily to add to their existing workloads. Vince had asked Head Office if they could send someone to Manchester to fill in for me. He had been told that no one was available at the moment but if someone became free they would agree to his request. Vince knew from experience that no help would be forthcoming and that he and the others would have to cope.

And here was I on a Friday, in Cyprus and being paid for gardening!

I was still pretty hyper as I had been working late for days to leave my files in a state where someone else could take them over plus I had endured the trauma of driving to London, the long flight into the unknown and leaving Ann behind. I somehow had to calm down.

We enjoyed a pleasant breakfast of Cyprus orange juice, delicious bread, which Alison had just bought from a local general store, and a choice of sliced ham or marmalade. There was freshly percolated coffee gurgling away on one of the kitchen worktops.

The back door was wide open and I saw the relatively small wasteland which Roger and I were to transform into a garden.

The bungalow was new and had two bedrooms, a lounge (a corner of which was, "the office"), a kitchen with dining facilities and a bathroom. It wasn't big by any stretch of the imagination but was lovely. It had a flat roof and was painted white, the windows and doors being in natural wood. It was Number 8 Kalypsos Street, Acropolis, Nicosia, Cyprus and would become my part time sanctuary over the next twelve weeks.

We two highly qualified gardeners worked in incredible heat moving barrow loads of earth from the pile in the road to the back garden. Alison was concerned about our well being and kept us supplied with orange squash.

Once the job was done we all piled into the car and travelled about 15 miles to the garden centre.

The place had a good selection of garden tools and equipment, lots of different styles of terracotta pots, barbecues, clay ovens and a fine selection of garden plants appropriate to the climate. Roger let Alison get on with her plant and shrub selection whilst the two of us wandered about the centre chatting about T & H and the various members of staff whom we knew. I didn't know any of the overseas people who he mentioned and of my contacts he only knew Vincent.

Following payment and the consuming of ice lollies, we loaded the car and returned to the bungalow. Roger and I were very dirty and sweaty so we each took a shower as Alison prepared lunch.

We enjoyed Cypriot cheeses, including feta, which I had never tasted before, ham and salami, salad, fresh bread, warm from the oven and my first bottle of the fantastic local beer, Keo. We also, naughtily, shared a bottle of Othello full-bodied red, Cypriot wine, such lunchtime debauchery, according to Roger being,

"In celebration of James's arrival!"

What an excuse! What a treat!

I felt rather sleepy thereafter but wasn't given an opportunity for a nap as Roger declared,

"Get your swimmers! We're off to the Hilton Club!"

We made our way in old Heinz to the Cyprus Hilton, the hotel describing itself as the "Gem of the Mediterranean... with magnificent views of the pool, gardens, Nicosia and the Kyrenia mountains." It further boasted to having... "150 air-conditioned rooms". "Oh, to be in one of them right now," I thought.

The hotel was but a short drive from Kalypsos Street and I was made a temporary member of the Hilton Swimming and Sports Club. What an afternoon! Swimming, drinking Keo beer and sunbathing. And still being paid!

That evening we had a barbecue in the back garden then played Scrabble.

We had enjoyed a few drinks and had a laugh over the choice of words, some of which were rude and were not allowed!

One word, which wasn't rude, started life as Cove, then developed to Cover, then onto Discover, from where it became Rediscover leading to my coup de grace of (wait for it)... Rediscoverer.

"What the hell is a Rediscoverer?" yelled a slightly merry Roger.

"It's a person who discovers the same thing twice!" I yelled back.

"Can't have it!" yelled Roger.

"Fair enough!" I yelled back, and Alison said in a calm, yet authoritative voice...... "Bed!"

The following morning Roger gave me two files to read with a view to me giving my view as to how to progress the claims toward settlement.

There was a neat little desk and filing cabinet in a corner of the lounge so I parked myself there and waded through the papers. The desk faced a window from where I could watch the comings and goings of the street.

Neither of the claims were Cypriot nor Lebanese. Roger held a regional role with T & H and travelled the length and breadth of the Middle East dealing with all kinds of claims.

The first file that I read related to a loss of sight claim where there was a potential £50,000 at risk. It was suspected that the claimant wasn't blind at all but had bribed a doctor in Tehran to issue a certificate confirming that following an accident the claimant had lost sight in both eyes.

Basically all I could advise was that we should insist that the claimant to be examined by a specialist of our choice.

I went to find Roger who was sunbathing in the back garden providing, as men do, supervision for Alison, as she arranged and watered the last of her newly acquired plants.

"Roger I have read the loss of sight claim file and..."

"Stop you there James. Sorry I shouldn't have bothered you with that one. We received a telex last week to say that the claimant was accidentally shot dead at a Bedouin wedding reception that he was attending.

Some of the guests took to horse following the ceremony and were firing rifles into the air when a ricocheting bullet went straight through his right eye and into his brain. Poetic justice eh?

Hey you've just reminded me. We can submit our fee invoice on that file as the case is now closed! Can you draft a Final Report for me based on the info on the file please? I'll calculate the fee. Good work young man.

Now on another subject. Do you have your dinner suit and bits and bobs with you?" he enquired. God who does he think I am? Why should I have brought my dinner suit to the Middle East?

"No Roger, a bit remiss of me, but I didn't bring my dinner suit and bits and bobs," I retorted with more than a hint of sarcasm.

"Shame. What it is, is that we are invited by pals Ron and Libby to attend a "do" organised by the United Kingdom Citizens' Association to celebrate Her Majesty's Silver Jubilee, it being 25 years since the death of her father in 1952, and of her accession to the throne. Here's the invitation.... silver print on good quality card. Let me read a bit to you and Alison." He called for Alison to join us. She sat beside me on the settee and he started to read out the content of the invitation,

"A Night To Remember to celebrate the Silver Jubilee of Her Majesty, Queen Elizabeth II at 7.30pm on Saturday the 18th June 1977 at the Hotel and Catering Institute of Nicosia. Champagne reception, the Ceremony of Beating the Retreat by the band and Corps of Drums of the 3rd Battalion Royal Anglian Regiment, Buffet dinner followed by dancing. Carriages at 12.30am."

And boy can these folk dance! The regimental band, who are based at Episkopi garrison, are providing the music for the dancing. I've heard them before. They are excellent. Get everyone dancing! Ballroom, trad jazz, modern jazz, rock and roll... the lot! What have you got that you can wear?" he enquired.

"I have brought a light weight mohair two piece suit in beige, and have a white shirt, brown tie and brown suede desert boots. Will that do?"

"It'll have to, won't it!" he laughed.

The time came for us to attend the function, Roger and Alison resplendent in dinner jacket and ball-gown, and me looking more like an extra from Lawrence of Arabia than the attendee of a "posh do!"

We arrived at the venue and I felt very much out of place. There were big limousines pulling up some with drivers and what looked to me like Lords and Ladies stepping out of them. Medals, Chains of

Office and other appendages adorned many of the guests superb outfits.

Roger explained my clothing situation to our hosts and to our fellow table companions but I am pleased to say that, as the drink flowed, my lack of sartorial elegance seemed to become irrelevant, especially following the announcement from the Master of Ceremonies that, "Gentlemen have the President's permission to smoke and also have the President's permission, in view of the extreme of heat, to remove their jackets and if so desired, their bow ties."

I was roasting and was the first to de-jacket and remove my brown tie. I now considered myself to be suitably dressed in my white shirt and no tie, looking more or less like all the other male guests who flung themselves around the dance floor filled with celebratory cheer, nobody noticing my beige trousers and desert boots amongst the melee of jitterbugging black trouser legs!

I jived with ladies old enough to know better, encouraged by gin and tonic to throw themselves into high octane dance. I spun them round and hooted and hollered with the best of them.

Her Majesty would have been proud of her subjects in this far flung corner of the world.

I held an interesting yet alarming conversation with a large lady, the wife of a retired naval Commodore, who had bought a retirement home on Cyprus. She introduced herself to me as, Boomer

Featherstone, or that's what it sounded like through the slur of wine and gin,

"You a fwend of Woger?" she boomed over the bandsmen who were blasting out the closing bars of the Hokey Cokey.

"Yes and no. I work for the same firm as Woger and have been seconded to help him sort out the Beirut office following the troubles," I shouted back.

"Oh my Gawd! You poor thing! Don't go to Beirut! It's still bloody dangerous don'tcha know! Well must dash I pwomised Julian that I would partner him in The Gay Gordon's and they've just struck up the music. Toodle-pip."

She staggered away to find poor Julian, whoever he was, and I thought, "Well thanks a lot Boomer, you've really cheered me up!"

All good things come to an end and thus, following a boisterous rendition of God Save The Queen, we all toddled off home. We were sensibly being taxied on that evening both to and from the event.

On the way back to the bungalow I told Roger and Alison what Boomer had said about Beirut and Roger replied,

"Yes it can be dangerous, but the secret is to keep a low profile, and to respect the curfew absolutely."

"Curfew!?" I squeaked.

I heard Alison mutter to herself, "Oh my God."

Roger continued, "Yes it's 10pm till sunrise. There's no police force at the moment, just the Syrian peace keeping force who are there to try to maintain law and order and to protect folk like us. You'll see their soldiers all over the place. They are friendly enough to foreigners but as I say, just keep a low profile."

I sat for a minute in silence then thought that I would change the subject,

"By the way. Why is Mrs Featherstone called Boomer?" Alison replied, as she knew her through the church and the bridge club.

"Oh it all stems from her university days where she met and captured her first of four husbands.

She went out with him for a while but he found someone else so he "chucked" her. She persisted and they were a couple again for a while but then he "chucked" her again.

This happened about five times but each time he "chucked" her she came back and re-claimed him. She eventually married the poor blighter and thus she earned the nickname Boomerang, which was shortened to Boomer.

None of our crowd know her Christian name."

"Right," I said, realising that I had just been part of a world in which I was an alien.

The taxi dropped us off and after a quick coffee we were soon in our beds.

I lay on my back for a while with my hands behind my head staring at the ceiling and going over in my mind the events of the last few days which, of course, included the surreal celebration of Her Majesty's Silver Jubilee, which I considered myself to have been very privileged to have attended.

The following morning during breakfast, with the three of us nursing thick heads, Roger warned me that the following day we were both flying to Beirut. In the meantime we were off into the Troodos mountains for lunch and a swim at The Forest Park Hotel!

It was quite a long and uncomfortable journey once we had left the main road, the majority of the roads in the mountains being unmade, rutted and dusty.

I was pleased to be a passenger, on my own in the rear of the car, watching the beautiful Cypriot countryside pass by. It was somewhat barren and dry but the hills and the pine trees presented me with memorable images enhanced by the wonderful scent of pine and herbs which wafted through the open windows.

Roger and Alison very kindly treated me to a fantastic lunch of foods which were new to me and included houmous, olives, taramasalata and pitabread followed by a rich beef stew with herbs called stifado, and glorious chipped Cyprus potatoes deep fried in olive oil.

I loved everything about the meal including the view from our table overlooking the pool area with the pine clad hills of Mount Olympus beyond. We quaffed a couple of bottles of Aphrodite white wine between us and then took a swim in the outdoor pool.

The journey back was uneventful, although a little tense, as Alison was a terrible passenger and was sure that some Cypriot lunatic driver would kill us! I had to agree that some of the driving skills and the risks that were taken were pretty scary. Being overtaken on blind bends several times on the journey for example.

I had seen, and Alison had pointed out, several makeshift roadside shrines where there had been terrible accidents.

Much to my and Alison's, relief we arrived back at the bungalow in one piece, the last several miles having been driven in pitch darkness, which made driving even more risky.

We sat and chatted for a while drinking most welcome glasses of chilled Keo beer, eventually saying our "Good-nights" just before mid-night.

And so I plodded off contentedly to bed.

I had enjoyed three days of paid "fun in the sun", but as I tried to sleep, I experienced deep, uneasy feelings about flying to Beirut in the morning.

Out Of The Frying Pan.....

So the day had arrived and on Monday 20th June 1977, leaving a sad looking Alison behind at the bungalow, Roger and I took a taxi to Larnaca airport for the 3pm Middle East Airlines flight ME262 for Beirut. The flight takes only about 30 minutes.

Once we had settled into our seats Roger handed to me the first and second parts of a paper which he had prepared as part of a dossier which we were to append to our claim reports to the various insurers who had instructed us to deal with property damage and loss of profit claims arising from the troubles.

He closed his eyes and was soon asleep. I began to read the paper.

1.   General

Lebanon is a small country of some 2,400 square miles with a coastline on the Eastern Mediterranean stretching for some eighty miles. It's chief coastal towns and ports are Beirut, the capital city in the centre of the Country, with Tripoli in the north and Sidon in the south. A range of mountains rises steeply from the narrow coastal plain behind which lies the fertile plain of the Bekaa valley. The centre of the agricultural industry is situated here at Zahleh. A second mountain range lies beyond which forms the natural boundary with neighbours Syria in the north and east. Israel borders the southern side.

2. Population

The population comprises a variety of indigenous clans or tribes of varying Christian and Moslem sects together with refugee elements of yesteryear mainly Kurds, Armenians and other political exiles. It is a polyglot. The latest unofficial population statistics published under confessional status are as follows:-

Moslem Shi'ites	970,000
Moslem Sinnis	690,000
Moslem Druzes	342,000
Christian Maronites	496,000
Greek Orthodox	230,000
Roman Catholics	213,000
Others Un-stated	

3. Beirut

Beirut, often referred to as The Playground of the Middle East due to it's abundance of luxury hotels, cafes, restaurants, designer retail establishments and casinos, has for some years enjoyed the status of the financial and commercial centre for the region being strategically placed with good communications and living conditions for foreign residents and as a summer resort for the region owing to its more temperate climate.

"Beirut sounds great! I hope he's got his facts right." But the truth of the situation, following the current end of the troubles in this land, was far from this rose tinted glasses, travel brochure view.

The second part of Roger's paper incorporated 43 foolscap pages documenting the events leading up to the troubles and the key events during those times, information which he and his assistant, Yussef, had gleaned from newspaper, television and radio reports.

It read, that whilst serious unrest between the various factions had been brewing up for sometime, there was a major turning point when, on the 13th April 1975 members of the Phalangist Militia (a private, right wing army of the largest political party) ambushed a bus carrying a group of Palestinian commandos. It was reported that 26 Palestinians, 2 Phalangists and 2 others were killed.

Thereafter the problems escalated apace and lasted well over a year. Over 25,000 people were reported to have been killed and some 40,000 injured. Property damage in the major centres was extremely heavy.

God, it must have been awful. All those people dead and injured and tens of thousands of families' lives affected forever.

The plane commenced it's descent to Beirut International Airport and Roger awoke.

We walked into heat even more intense than that of Cyprus and, upon entering the arrivals area, I was immediately conscious of a fairly substantial military presence. We were soon through border control where my visa was carefully scrutinised and were met by Yussef, who was effectively in charge of the office when Roger was away. I liked him at once.

He was about forty years of age and my height with slicked black hair and with flashes of gold showing from his front teeth. He seemed a happy soul. He was smoking and as I discovered, like most of his countrymen, all but chain smoked. He had a gruff smokers voice, which made me want to cough for him, and spoke excellent English.

We made our way to his car, which was a huge but not very new, rust coloured Cadillac... with air conditioning! I had never been in such a long car nor one with such floating suspension. The ride made me feel that I was on the sea not land. Neither had I experienced air conditioning before, and it was most welcome. Yussef pointed out that using it greatly increased the petrol consumption and Roger in a tired, "we've been here before," kind of voice reminded him that the firm paid all his petrol bills.

As we left the airport car park I could see the city in the distance and was shocked to see two columns of smoke rising dramatically into the sky.

"What's all that smoke about? Has there been more trouble?" I nervously asked. Yussef laughed and said,

"Don't worry James. There has been no refuse collection for a very long time now so neighbourhoods have occasional bonfires to get rid of the stuff!"

"Thank God for that. I was ready to get the next plane back to Cyprus!"

We were driving along a dual carriageway and every now and then there were Syrian forces checkpoints. Roger said to say nothing unless spoken to and just show passports to the soldiers when asked. I have to admit that the soldiers seemed friendly enough and were chatting amongst themselves with plenty of laughter and loads of smoking.

We entered the outskirts of the city and I became aware of what I can only describe as desolation and deprivation. There were plenty of burnt out shops and businesses and I saw people camping in derelict buildings and makeshift camps. The city centre seemed a bit more normal with day to day life carrying on as best it could. There were fruit and veg stalls on the street sides and quite a number of shops, businesses and cafes were open for trade. Roger spoke,

"Take us to the office first would you please Yussef."

"Certainly, Roger," said a compliant Yussef.

I had read in the firm's literature that the office was in The Verdun Centre on the Rue Verdun and was pleasantly surprised to find it to be a modern, multi-tenanted, six storey office block with shops in the ground floor area.

Only two of the shops were occupied, one being a café with a "takeaway." This facility proved to be most welcome and much used by little old me, the favourite cure for a wee hangover being a ham, cheese and gherkin toastie and a bottle of cola. The other shop was occupied by a newsagent, who also sold sweets and tobacco products, which I found to be similarly useful. Of the several offices in The Centre we were one of only three tenants currently in occupation.

We parked the Cadillac in the basement car park and travelled by lift to the fifth floor. It was after office hours the idea being for Roger to see what had taken place in his absence, and for me to see the place.

They were nice bright modern offices comprising one large general office with two smaller rooms adjoining, a galley kitchen and our own lavatory and wash hand basin.

The views from the windows were fantastic! I could see right over the city centre including views of the very badly damaged Hilton Hotel and the equally badly damaged Holiday Inn. In the distance was the reassuring sight of the Mediterranean Sea.

The corner windows of the general office were broken the remaining shards of glass being held together by gaffer tape and sheets of cardboard. Yussef explained,

"During the time that the office was abandoned, a rocket went through one corner window and out the other! We will have to wait some time for a repair as the landlord says there is no suitable glass available at the moment. We are on his list of jobs to be done. God willing!"

"So be it!" I added.

Roger finished his brief look through correspondence which had accumulated since his last visit and Yussef drove us to the Mayflower Hotel off Hamra Street in the city centre.

The hotel was fine and I was introduced to the reception staff as their new, long staying guest. My room 605 on the sixth floor was more than adequate and included en suite facilities, a television and a small balcony overlooking the street.

Roger and I ordered a light snack in the hotel bar, The Duke of Wellington, and I tasted my first Campari and soda, which Roger said I should try. I liked it and enjoyed many over the next three months. Complimentary nibbles were always on the bar and comprised carrots, cut lengthways in thin slices in a vinaigrette dressing and pistachio nuts. I had never had either of them before and consumed them with gusto between slurps of drink and puffs of smoke!

In order that I would look as cool and trendy as some of the beautiful Lebanese bar dwellers, I purchased a pack of twenty Gitanes French cigarettes and a box of Fire Prince matches ...."The Arsonists Choice" ... ; an advertising logo created of my very own fertile imagination!

The following morning after a decent breakfast, Yussef picked us up and I started my first proper day of work.

The day started badly when Roger said he wanted to have a chat,

"James," he paused for a few seconds and fiddled with his very nice stainless steel Parker fountain pen, which I later established he had purchased tax free and at a very good price from a souk in Dhahran, "Alison and I have to go back to England next week, partially to catch up with a backlog of leave which is owed to me and to sort out some personal business."

He seemed embarrassed and a little coy and I realised that Mr Harrup would have known about this all along when he seduced me to take this temporary assignment. I was not prepared for the next bit though.

"We will be away for between six and eight weeks. Is that ok?" Bloody hell! I'm to be on my own and in charge for most of my time in this, not so long ago, war zone! I had never managed an office before, I thought, as I fiddled with my not very nice turquoise-barrelled Bic Clic pen which I had purchased from a newsagents in Chorley.

"God Roger that's a shock," I whimpered,"I thought I was asked to come here to help out, not to be responsible!"

"Bear something in mind James. The office is all but dead, so you wont be rushed off your feet, as you are in Manchester. You are here effectively to "mind the shop" so to speak. You are earning a tax free bonus with all expenses paid and, if you show the partners that you do a good job, it will be a feather in your cap for the future. Plus the firm will pay for flights to and from Cyprus five or six times during your tour of duty for, let's say, two or three day breaks at Kalypsos Street. What do you think?"

"It's a bit of a shock, but you are here for the rest of the week so, hopefully, I should have time to pick your brain about one or two things and to familiarise myself with the office and with Beirut," I replied.

"Great! You've met Yussef, now come and meet Josette and Salim."

I was introduced to a very pleasant middle aged, auburn haired, Lebanese lady who was the office secretary and to young Salim who was the office junior and, as I noticed as the weeks went by, seemed to be Yussef's slave!

"Saleeeem!" Yussef would shout. "Yes please Mista Yussef," he would sweetly reply. "Go and get me 20 Rothmans King Size Tipped Cigarettes, a toasted cheese and onion sandwich and a can of lemonade, and see if Mister James desires anything before you go."

Yussef did try to be a little bossy with me, but basically we got on pretty well. I think he resented me being there and thought that he could have managed the place during Roger's extended absence.

The turning point came when he saw my Manchester business cards which I had "accidentally" left on Roger's desk. He had spotted the fact that I was qualified both in the Insurance Institute exams and in those of the Institute of Chartered Loss

Adjusters. This immediately placed me on a pedestal and made my life in the office somewhat easier.

Yussef could have entered the exams as an overseas member of the Insurance Institute but never took advantage of the opportunity.

The other two members of staff were smashing and during my stay both of them looked after me. Salim treated me like royalty and couldn't have been more helpful. Josette mothered me somewhat, which was particularly useful when I had stomach upsets or was feeling under the weather.

Everything here was so different from the frantic pace of Manchester office. I established that Beirut office only received 30 new instructions in 1976 and altogether there were only 58 claims on the books, many of which had not even been looked at!

In Manchester I would have at least 100 claims on the go at any one time and there would be about 500 active claim files in the office.

After I had taken a general look at the state of the cases I suggested to Roger that I should read through all the files over a period of time and draft an action plan for each claim highlighting what work had to be done to push them toward a settlement. I further recommended the preparation of an interim fee invoice for each of the cases, for the work carried out to date, to generate some income for Beirut office. Roger was impressed,

"Well done James! That's the spirit! I'm just off to meet a pal of mine who is in the city for a few days.

See you later," he said. Yussef shouted to Roger from his adjoining office, "I will drive you. I need to collect some dry cleaning for my wife."

And off the two of them went leaving me to "get on with it"! It was a bit like a scene from a sitcom! I sat there "like cheese at fourpence," with dropped jaw, watching them shuffle quickly out of the office, like two naughty little boys! But it didn't bother me one little bit. It made me smile. I was in a pleasant office with decent colleagues, with time on my hands to study the files and plan what action was required on each claim, and Josette had just brought me a coffee and a plate of biscuits!

The majority of the files related to massive war damage claims involving hotels, department stores, warehouses, factories, motor car showrooms and all manner of businesses. From what I could read they all seemed to be total losses. Yussef had visited about 75% of the locations and had taken brief notes and all important photographs. On only one claim had he actually met the insured party, as the other owners had quit Lebanon for their own safety, and had not yet returned. They had, however, lodged claims which we were now looking at for the insurance companies. There was no pressure on us as the policyholders were abroad and nobody was chasing!

My plan was to prepare an interim report on each claim and to enclose a copy of Roger's general report on how the situation had escalated, including the key events during the "troubles", together with a series of mounted photographs to illustrate the damage, on the basis that, a picture paints a thousand words. Each report would include an interim fee invoice to cover our work to date.

This process took several weeks and included Yussef driving me to some of the claim sites so that I could get a "feel" for what I was writing about.

The exercise was most successful and to both Roger's and the partner's delight, I produced interim fee invoices in the order of £35,000 over the period.

All of these were paid because Yussef and I jointly hand delivered the reports to the local insurance company offices and said that we could not release the reports to them unless they paid our fee upfront! None of the companies objected as they needed the reports for their Head Offices to establish if the claims were covered under a Riot and Civil Commotion extension to policies which had been granted when the troubles started, or whether they were not covered, in view of a War Damage exclusion. The work was interesting and I paced myself, taking much more time on each file than I would do back in the UK.

When I arrived the office hours were 8am to 2pm and 5pm to 7.30.However in July "Summer Hours" arrived and work was from 8am till 2pm only! This was due to the summer temperatures which were regularly 100 degrees Fahrenheit and over.

Socially I was pretty much on my own, although when Roger was around we spent time together and

Yussef and his family were very kind in having me round for lunch or dinner from time to time. On a couple of occasions they took me away for the weekend to their bungalow in the mountains to escape the heat of the city.

I also became a regular attendee at the several cinemas in the city where the films were changed at least twice a week. It was odd sitting there on my own in the dark but pleasantly comforting to be taken away for a couple of hours into the fantastic land of the movie.

The most memorable film that I saw, and which is now in my top ten favourites was, The Man Who Would Be King, starring Sean Connery and Michael Caine.

"Of coursh we can make it Peachy. Itsh only bloody shnow!"

If I was in Beirut over a weekend I would wander down to the seafront area of the city and watch amateur football matches. I sometimes got chatting with folk, which was enjoyable, but for much of my "free" time I was on my own.

Most days after work I would spend the afternoon at the hotel where there was a small rooftop swimming pool with half a dozen sun-beds around it.

There was a hotel phone by the pool, from where I could order food and drink, and it became an in-house joke that when Mister James phoned down from the roof they were to bring mushroom omelette and chips and a pint or three of lager! It was pretty good up there and there were shady areas when needed.

Now and again I was joined by other guests, mainly British men over on business. I also met some chaps who worked for the BBC one of whom I had seen on TV news programmes over the years. I also befriended some evening regulars in the hotel's Duke of Wellington bar where we drank and smoked and chatted about this that and the other.

One who became a pal was the editor of The Middle East Digest and was from Blackpool. He was called Harry Butterworth and was a great support to me when I was feeling a bit down and lonely. It was Harry who got me into trouble!

We had been to a steak house called, The Captain's Cabin, a regular haunt of mine where I would often dine alone, and would consume very nice peppered steak and chips, three or four beers and a couple of glasses of wine.

We left "The Cabin" at about 9pm and Harry invited me back to his flat for a nightcap. We chatted and laughed and joked and time passed.

"Harry! Bloody hell it's eleven o'clock! The curfew!" I shouted. Harry laughed, "Don't fret. You're not that late. If you get stopped say you're sorry, grovel a bit, and you should be ok," he tried to reassure.

"Have you ever been out during curfew?" His response of, "Not bloody likely!" did nothing to make me feel any better about my predicament. As I left Harry shouted, "You'll be fine. Let me know how you get on."

I set off for The Mayflower, which was only about a quarter of a mile away, and found the streets to be eerily quiet. In the distance, and on the opposite footpath, I became aware of a pack of nine stray dogs lying in a group and all looking very interested in me! "Shit," I said under my breath.

I had been told that packs of previously domesticated pets had been roaming free as a result of the troubles and that many carried the rabies virus. I went hot and cold with fear. What would Commander James Bond say to the gorgeous damsel by his side when faced with this situation? Ah yes, I know.

"Just act normally and don't be frightened as they can schmell fear and will eat you." Don't be frightened or they'll eat you! Double shit!! My mind was racing.

"That's what I'll do, just keep walking at the same pace in a nonchalant manner, stay calm and pretend you haven't seen them," I mumbled under my breath.

Out of the corner of my left eye I saw the dogs rise to their feet one by one and the biggest one, which I presumed to be the leader, started to cross the road toward me! I want my mammy. How could this be happening to me? I had a mental image of the newspaper headline.

At that moment I reached the street corner and on turning right to follow the pavement bumped into two members of the Syrian Peacekeeping Force enjoying a fag.

"Kill those dogs!!" I screamed.

They laughed and shooed the wild pack away by shouting and waving their rifles. I was ashen and sweating like a pig as one of them spoke.

"You should not be on the streets at this time. Do you not know about the curfew?"

"Yes I do and I am so sorry. I was visiting a friend and time went by so quickly that I left his flat a little late. I am so, so sorry," I grovelled, as recommended by Harry.

After taking my name and the name of the place where I was staying and noting Harry's name and address, they told me to be more careful in future, and not to breach the curfew. I can promise you, dear reader, that I never did breach that bloomin' curfew again!

As I walked away and neared the sanctuary of the hotel I could still hear their laughter.

Two other scary moments took place, the first when I was sunning myself by the hotel's rooftop pool when I heard machine gun fire in the street below. Being an un-James Bond type I rushed in fear to my hotel room and pushed the chest of drawers against the door. I sat somewhat numbed on the bed for a while staring at the door and feeling the colour draining from my face.

After about half an hour of no further gunfire I made my way down to Reception where all seemed normal. I enquired of Georges the bar manager as to what had taken place and he said,

"Some poor soul has gone to meet his maker. This is just one more of many retaliations that have taken place since things calmed down. You shoot my brother, and I will shoot you, is the order of the day I am afraid," he bellowed theatrically, shaking his fists in the air to emphasise the point. I nodded and returned to my sunbathing with a pint of lager. It's a mad and crazy world was all that I could think.

The second incident occurred when Yussef and I went to have another look and to take more photographs of a burnt out warehouse which had been a cold store for a variety of fruits. To our surprise the owner happened to be there and a dialogue followed.

He was a sweet looking, sad faced, small, plump man with a round face and an almost bald head. He was sitting on a low wall facing his burnt out business fidgeting with his worry beads. He asked what we were doing and Yussef explained that we were the loss adjusters acting on behalf of his insurers, and that I was Mister James from the London Office, which of course was untrue but sounded impressive.

He introduced himself as Mister Salah and spoke in good English, presumably for my sake.

"I am glad to meet you. Some of my friends tell me that these claims will not be paid. Is this true?" he enquired in a sad tone of voice. Yussef jumped in feet first, as was his style.

"There has been a war! What do you people expect!"

At that point the worry beads were thrown to the ground and with venom in his voice and with a pistol drawn from his trouser pocket Mr Salah screamed,

"I will shoot you and then I will shoot myself! I have invested all I have in this business, so if I am to lose all, I may as well become a murderer!"

I was dumbstruck. Fortunately, Yussef, being the older head and knowing the Lebanese psyche, intervened,

"You fool. What will you gain? Mister James and I have not yet written our report in respect of your claim. There is every possibility that your claim MAY be paid. If you shoot us then how can we make a report?"

This tactic wouldn't have worked in certain districts of Manchester, but Yussef seemed to have done the trick as Mr Salah burst into tears, picked up his worry beads and returned the gun to his trouser pocket.

"Now my friend," said Yussef, putting an arm around him. "Allow me and Mister James to get back to the office to make our report on this terrible destruction of your business, and upon your unfortunate situation, and, as soon as possible, you WILL hear something from our office."

Brilliant! Within seconds of death one minute and now shaking hands and waving to the sad figure as we drove back to the city centre.

We had travelled in silence for a couple of minutes when, out of the blue, Yussef screamed at the top of his voice and to no one in particular, "Bloody Hell! That was close! "

On the general side of things I had noticed that 90% of the cars which charged around the city, oblivious of the law or to those occasional traffic lights which were still working, were semi-wrecks, many without windows, and lots with bullet holes through the bodywork!

Every day I was witnessing damage and destruction all around.

There were quite a few beggars on the streets and some folk were living in what can only be described as wood and cardboard shanty towns. The majority of the beggars were children, all maimed in some way, many with horrific injuries not necessarily caused accidentally.

One poor lad whom I often saw was without legs and transported himself along on a home made cart made from planks of wood on what looked like a child's push chair chassis.

I had been warned that he and some others were "owned" by unscrupulous adults who forced them to beg from foreigners to bring in some income.

Without drawing attention to myself I had observed these people lurking in the shadows, keeping an eye on the beggars, to ensure that they were putting heart and soul into their begging and to further ensure that they were not pocketing some of the money. It was appalling, but such was life in Beirut at that time.

Days back in Cyprus were bliss and, as Roger promised, I travelled back there six times during my three month tour of duty.

Each time I landed at Larnaca old Heinz, the yellow Renault 5, would be sitting waiting for me in the baking sun covered in dust and sand.

"Windows open... and off we go... over the mountains to Kalypsos Street," I cheerfully shouted to Heinz, to the surprise of two chaps collecting their car nearby, who were trying to see to whom I was talking. I called out to them as I drove past their pale blue Morris Minor 1000cc.

"It's the heat you know!" Giving them the treat of one of my famous lunatic faces with the Harry Secombe voice. The one with the tongue lolling out of distorted mouth complemented by bulging eyes.

"We know the feeling!" they yelled back as me and my buddy Heinz zoomed out of the car park waving to anybody who was looking.

Most of my time on the island was spent reading files and making notes ,reading a collection of books and magazines in the bungalow, attending to gardening watering duties fearful of Alison's rage if anything which she planted had died, listening to Roger and Alison's Bang and Olufsun super music centre, washing Heinz and generally pottering about.

I coveted that B & O music centre having nothing remotely like it at home. It incorporated a radio, a record player and a cassette player/recorder all in one!

I went through R & A's record collection becoming a new fan of Herbert Von Karajan, bouzouki music and Simon and Garfunkel. I bought a couple of blank cassettes tapes, which at the time were expensive, but cheaper than the records, from a shop in Nicosia and recorded my favourites to take back home.

Of the Von Karajan tracks my favourite was Wolfie Mozart's short yet haunting Ave, verum corpus(K.618), which the little genius composed for a Corpus Christi service just six months before his death. It was truly spiritual and I thought would be a great piece to have as background music whilst making gentle love. Not like my pal Keith Fish who once tried to make love to the Flight of the Bumble Bee from Tsar Saltan by Rimsky-Korsakov and ended up in traction or my Roman Catholic pal Morris Tanner who tried the same idea to Jake The Peg by Rolf Harris and suffered a slipped disc. Ah the joys of the rhythm method!

Of the bouzouki music I found that, apart from the irritating Theme from Zorba the Greek (another tune not to make love to), anything by Mikis Theodorakis was splendid and conjured up the image of balmy evenings sitting in a seafront taverna sipping wine and watching the sun sink into the aquamarine horizon.

My particular favourite was one that Mikis co-wrote with Iakovos Kampanellis entitled Strose To Stroma Sou which means Lay Your Bed. Funnily enough, I discovered that the opening bars to this lovely tune were the same as the beginning of Zorba, but instead of heading for a maniacal crescendo, the music drifts beautifully along at the pace of a Cypriot widow riding her donkey from the olive groves to home following a morning's labour.

Of the Simon and Garfunkel my favourite was The Boxer. I loved everything about it, particularly the atmosphere Paul Simon created from such an unusual subject,

"In the clearing stands a boxer
And a fighter by his trade
And he carries the reminders
Of every glove that laid him down
Or cut him till he cried out
In his anger and his pain
I am leaving, I am leaving
But the fighter still remains."

Fantastic!

I was still a temporary member of the Hilton Swimming and Sports Club and once or twice went there for a swim and a sunbath.

I was not very comfortable on my own, as for years there had always been Ann by my side. I decided not to go back following an incident of misunderstanding which left me embarrassed and not wishing to return.

I was blissfully lying on a sun bed following a swim when I became conscious of my nearest fellow sun-worshipper, a rather large busty lady in a swimsuit, who was throwing pieces of a bread roll to some birds which flitted about the pool area. She was possibly hard of hearing and I worked out that she was most probably Germanic as she coo-eed the birdies with more volume that seemed appropriate.

"Come along you birdies and eat zee bread. It vill make you strong. Come on. Come on," she shouted to the annoyance of some of the other Hiltonites. She came back to her sun bed which was in touching distance of mine and to my dismay spoke to me,

"Zees little birds are charming I sink. Yah?" she shouted.

"Yes. They are very pretty," I said, hoping that would be it.

"Sorry, I can't hear you. I am a little deaf you see," she bellowed.

"Sorry. I said, yes, they are very pretty," I encored in a much louder voice, causing most of the other guests to look at us over the top of their books, newspapers and magazines. One chap twitched his Times broadsheet violently to emphasise his irritation.

"Vot are zee little ones mit zee long tails called?" she roared.

"Er, I think, if I am not mistaken, that they may be long tailed tits."

"Ah yah. Vee have these also in zee Rhineland. Also vee have zee blue tits , zee crested tits und zee bearded tits. Zere is another variety but I can't remember its name at zee moment," she spouted.

"No. I can't think of the name at the moment, but I am sure it will come to me," I replied, in an embarrassingly loud voice, hoping she was finished, and to be sure of an end to this saga, getting to my feet, collecting my belongings and saying as I walked away towards the pool area exit,

"Well I must be off. It has been nice meeting you."

"It has been very pleasant in meeting with you too also," she concluded.

If I had the power to turn back the clock there are many times in my life when I would have done so. What happened next was one of them. Why didn't I just keep on walking to the exit?

I had suddenly remembered the name of the wee birdie that we had missed from our list and turned around and shouted back to her,

"Great tits!"

Everyone around the pool naturally heard me and there were giggles aplenty when she bellowed back.

"Sank you very mutch. In my country zis is a very good compliment."

My face became scarlet with self conscious embarrassment as I stood in full view of the other guests. I quickly left the pool area and never returned!

During my "Cyclops" days it was a pleasant surprise to receive from Head Office two new Cypriot claims to investigate both of which were large fire claims which cleared my conscience somewhat at being there and not always being in Lebanon.

I had fallen in love with the local Keo beer and bought it in a wooden crate of 24 bottles from the local grocers shop, where I also purchased most of my foodstuffs, and would return the empties to receive a credit towards the next batch!

I had grown to love The Island of Aphrodite for the climate, the variety of scenery from beach to mountain, the history and in particular, the Greek Cypriot people.

Oh well, another Cypriot break was ending and so I got myself ready for the flight to Beirut, after first watering the garden plants, tidying the bungalow, making it secure, and plonking the empty Keo beer bottles in their crate before driving my pal Heinz once more over the mountains to Larnaca airport.

Roses of Grief

Back in Beirut, and heading for the end of my three months secondment, I was feeling much more confident in both my self esteem and my ability. I had grown in stature and, as one of the partners said following my repatriation to Blighty, I had been through a "character building" experience.

Dining out alone in Beirut was not easy and whilst I tried various restaurants I kept on returning to the Captain's Cabin where I got to know the waiter, Ahmed, a gentle young man whom I guessed had lost family and friends during the past few years.

We never discussed the events. Ahmed was more interested in chatting about the football teams of England's First Division, especially Manchester United, which suited me fine!

I was also emotionally moved by the nightly visits to The Cabin of a sad- looking old lady who sold individual red roses to the diners for one Lebanese pound. I felt sorry for her and, although I couldn't really afford it, purchased one most times that I saw her. She always smiled a "sad smile" and said in a distant voice, "Sank you verra mutz."

I wondered who she was and what was her story and, partly fuelled by vino and personal short-term loneliness, returned one night to The Mayflower and was inspired by her very existence to become a part time poet!

Roses of Grief (A Song For Lebanon)

Where does she come from?
Where does she go?
Nobody questions.
Nobody knows.
Bright bunch of roses held to her breast,
The blooms are offered, no one is pressed.

Her sons were martyred,
Brave boys and strong.
Her country ravaged,
Who's right who's wrong?
Are we so different? One olive leaf.
The lovely lady. Roses of grief

Why did they suffer?
Why did they die?
The blazing cedars,
Light up the sky.
A burning building, more souls to mourn.
The sound of battle, heralds the dawn.

Speak to me of good times
Not so long ago.
Tell me of the future,
Only God can know.
Death! The only victor, in this bloody race.
Tears of shame and passion, reflected in her face.

And so tomorrow.
What will there be?
Will there be rainbows over the sea?
Will beams of sunlight warm hearts beneath?
Or will she bring us....
Roses of grief?

Nearing the end of my secondment I was much more relaxed, I felt part of the Beirut "scene" and had fallen in love with Cyprus.

I was now a Cheshire Cat with Scottish blood, a robust Lancashire spirit and with the Greek Cypriot love of life!

Roger was now back for the last few weeks of my time in the region. He advised me that my flight home was booked on British Airways flight number BA489 for Sunday 18th September 1977. I asked him if I could phone Ann from the office phone and he agreed.

Calls to the UK were limited because of the cost and during my three months tour of duty I had only spoken with Ann on three other occasions. We had corresponded by mail, writing every few days to one another. I also exchanged correspondence with mum, Ann's parents and one or two of my pals.

Ann was thrilled to hear my voice and to have confirmation of my flight home details.

I had to advise her, however, that I would have to stay in London on the Sunday night, call into see Mr Harrup at the office on the Monday, pick up my new car and then drive it through the City of London and thereafter, hopefully, arrive home safe and sound on the Monday evening.

Although we had been married for eight years we were both very excited at the prospect of our reunion and the tax free bonus which I had more than earned.

Roger confirmed that he and Alison had agreed with the Partners that in about two months time he would be based back in London after 15 years in the Middle East, and that a new permanent Manager of the Beirut Office had been appointed. He would still be part of the overseas operation and would travel to specific large or complex international claims, mainly those in the Middle East, from his UK base as and when required.

The time came for me to say goodbye to Yussef, Josette and a weeping Salim, whom I promised to help to enrol in a correspondence course with the Chartered Insurance Institute when I got home. He was keen to progress his career as were many young Lebanese men and I wished him well in his endeavours.

Yussef drove Roger and me to Beirut International for my last flight to Cyprus. Heinz was awaiting our return, covered in sand and dust once again, and for the last time I drove us back to the bungalow. We were alone as Alison was still in England and so we drove into Nicosia that evening for a slap up, farewell, Chinese meal, washed down with Keo beer and Othello red wine.

The following morning I packed my briefcase and suitcase and following breakfast Roger ordered a taxi to take me to Larnaca airport.

"Well, James. I am really pleased, firstly to have met you and secondly, for all the great work which you have done. The office hasn't been so straight in years!"

"Hey, Roger, it's been a pleasure and quite an experience for someone whose career so far has been based in Lancashire. I would recommend a tour of duty abroad to anyone. Thanks for all you have done to help and look after me," I said, feeling a little choked.

"Don't be silly," he said, "It was my pleasure."

I whiled away a couple of hours reading the local paper and then walked around the garden checking that Alison's precious plants were fit and well and watering those which appeared to be in need.

When the taxi arrived Roger and I walked out to the front of the bungalow to the shrill sound of a chorus of cicadas filling the hot air. We finally shook hands, not realising that it would be several years before we would meet again at a Chartered Institute of Loss Adjusters annual dinner in London.

The taxi whisked me away to the airport and I sat quietly on the back seat breathing in the hot, herb-scented air through the open window, my mind running through the events of the past twelve weeks.

Home James

Everything went according to plan and the flight arrived at Heathrow airport just 15 minutes late.

I took a taxi to The White House Hotel and checked in with much more confidence than when Ann and I had checked in just three months previously. I was tired and after a meal in the Coffee Shop of delicious fish, chips and peas with a slice of lemon and a half bottle of Chablis, I retired to bed and slept like the proverbial log.

After breakfast it was hot foot to Finsbury Circus by cab to see Mr Jinks. For the record, in all the twenty six years that I worked for T & H, I could never bring myself to call Mr Harrup, "Jinks". It just didn't seem right.

Later in my career, whilst attending one of the Institute of Loss Adjusters annual dinners, which some rascal cleverly nicknamed The Fire Raiser's Ball, at the Grosvenor House Hotel on London's famous Park Lane, he pulled me to one side, both of us slightly worse for drink, and said,

"Now James, my dear old chap, it'sh about time you called me Jinksh. What?"

"Ok, Mishter Harrup. If you shay so, Mishter Harrup. It'sh a deal, sir!" I responded vacantly, giving him a hug, and then wandering off to the bar leaving him in fits of giggles, with vin rouge lapping over the edge of his wine glass and down his hand on its journey toward the cuff of his very expensive dress shirt.

So I arrived at the office and there was Moneypenny on Reception,

"Ah, James. Good to have you back. I believe you have done a sterling job?" she purred. I threw an imaginary hat onto the hat stand and wished that I could have said,

"Yesh Moneypenny. I shwarted Goldfinger'sh effortsh to take over the world'sh gold marketsh, and that evil Doctor No wont be causing anymore bother in the future." But instead I said, "Thanks. It was an experience and I'm glad that I seem to have done what was needed. Is Mr Harrup free?"

"Yes. Go on in. He's expecting you."

I made my way to the great man's office and knocked on the door. "Come on in James," roared the plummy home-counties voice. I entered as he was putting a golf ball into a practice "hole" with his umbrella handle. He got a hole in one.

"Did you see that? A fifteen footer. Not bad. What?" he boomed at the top of his voice and at the same time shaking my hand like a long lost friend.

"Sit down, sit down and tell me all about it!" he enthused.

For the next ten minutes I gave him a precis of what I had been doing and told him about the fees that my efforts had generated for the Beirut office.

"Yes, yes I know all about that. We didn't expect that! Bloomin' good show all round. Well done old chap. Now, your bonus of £1500 will be in your bank if you'd care to check.

Clifford arranged for it to be processed ready for your return so that you and the delightful Mrs B can now spend, spend, spend!

I don't think you will need to pay any income tax as the dosh was earned overseas, but, to be safe, have a word with Robbie in accounts and he will clarify. What?"

"Thank you very much. The extra money will indeed be most welcome and will help us to sort out one or two things," I replied, extremely relieved that the cash was safely in my bank. Jinks being the likeable rascal that he was had caused me to experience a bad dream in which he boomed at me,

"Bonus? Bonus? What bonus? What?"

But I was being a bit unfair in thinking that way as the truth was that both he and the other partners were good sorts.... if a little dippy and public-schoolboyish at times!

The extra money would truly be a fantastic bonus for Ann and me. We had been paying the minimum on our Access (Take The Waiting Out Of Wanting) credit card account for ages and we could now pay off the balance in full, buy some things that we needed for the house and stash a few bob away in our Halifax Building Society Liquid Gold savings account.

This was a turning point in our financial affairs, as from that time until now, we have always been in the black!

The sound of Mr Harrup's voice brought me round from my fiscal imaginings.

"Now then, old chap, I have the keys to your new car here and a map somewhere showing you how to find the multi-storey car park in which it sits awaiting it's new master! Let me see. Where did I put it? Oh here it is. It's the car park near London Bridge don't cha know. Here's the parking ticket. You'll have to pay when you leave. Got any cash on you?"

"Yes, thanks," I said rather nervously taking the keys, map and ticket from him.

"Well best of luck and see ya soon!" he replied.

"Mr Harrup. Sorry but what sort of car is it and do you have the registration number please?" I nervously asked, gaining the distinct feeling that I was quickly becoming an irritation to the great man.

"Oh, I don't know. Oh bother! I've to be at Lloyd's in ten minutes. Let me phone Clifford," he said as he dialled Cliff Clifford. I listened as he spoke and shouted to me to grab a pen and some paper.

"Ok Clifford, I'll shout it out," and in my direction, "Red Ford Capri... 1.6GL... Mark II... Registration number... KHS... 214... S. Now off you pop. I must get going," he said easing me gently toward the threshold of his office door.

"Thanks, Mr Harrup," I said to the closing door.

I collected my suitcase and briefcase from Moneypenny's reception area and set off from Finsbury Circus with map in hand. Blimey, it was a long walk with heavy baggage down Moorgate, then Prince's Street, then King William Street, then Arthur Street and finally to the car park near the Thames and London Bridge. "I didn't ask which blinking floor it was on!" I said to nobody in particular. Hey, a stroke of luck! After scouring the first floor for ten minutes I walked up the stairs to the second floor and, lo and behold, my gleaming new company car was looking straight at me.

A brand new Mark ll Capri. She was gorgeous! Absolutely gorgeous! And she was "mine", all "mine".

I remembered that when the Mark l Capri was launched in 1969, there was a two page colour spread of this new Ford beauty in some national newspapers. I bought the Daily Mail, took out the "poster", and pinned it to my bedroom wall never thinking that one day I would be the custodian of one.

I was so chuffed! There she was, Europe's answer to the iconic Ford Mustang or, as I later discovered, a Cortina in drag! A two door coupe, hatchback, cracker of a car in bright red livery with alloy wheels and with what appeared to be a 100 foot bonnet!

I opened the door and put my bags on the back seat and then adjusted the seat to suit my driving position. There was that new car smell. What is it? I reckon a combination of new carpet, new upholstery and in the case of this particular non luxury vehicle... plastic!

I turned the ignition key and my new baby kicked into action. Then I had a sickening feeling in my stomach. Where the heck is Lytham from here?

I drove to the payment point and settled the parking bill. There was no one behind me so I asked the, hopefully, kindly attendant to point me in the right direction for Lytham St Anne's.

"St Ives. That's in yer Corwall init?" he kindly enquired.

"Sorry. No. You must have misheard me, I said Lytham St Anne's in Lancashire."

"Aw, that's amazing! I got an aunt what lives in Lanarkshire. She's Scotch y'know," he responded brightly.

I resisted the temptation of answering, from the frustrated Scottish part of me, that Scotch is a drink not a nationality....but I refrained, and knowing that Lanarkshire was north of where I wanted to go, complied with the confusion by saying,

"Oh that's great. Can you point me in the right direction for Lanarkshire please?"

"Easy. Go out of 'ere and turn right and you'll see a sign what says "To The Norf." Follow it till you see anovver sign what says, "To The Norf,"exeterra, exeterra, till you get to yer Lanarkshire, and say 'ello to me auntie. The best of luck to ya!"

"Brilliant! Thanks very much," I said, as I drove out of the car park trying to see over the long bonnet.

He was right with his directions, and although the traffic was heavy, I was able to follow the aforementioned signs and after only one hiccup of going around a massive roundabout near a massive park three times, because I became trapped in a lane, I eventually found myself on the M1 which I knew would lead me onto the M6 and thereafter, to the North West of England.

The Capri incorporated a radio as standard and once on the motorway I tuned to BBC Radio 2. The first tune was Ma Baker by Bony M, the sound of which took me back to one of the cinemas in Beirut which I used to frequent and which seemed to only own this one record, which was played continuously during the interval.

Beirut and Cyprus suddenly seemed millions of miles away as did all of my adventures.

The journey was pretty straight forward and I stopped at a couple of service stations for comfort breaks and to fill up with petrol.

Eventually I was leaving the M6 and driving through Preston and to home!

Home! I couldn't believe it. Here I was after three months away passing the Lytham landmark of the Land Registry Offices, followed by the famous expanse of grass known as Lytham Green; then past the iconic Lytham windmill and the equally iconic White Church, where I had been married eight years before, and then there I was turning the Capri onto our drive.

I turned off the engine and sat quietly for a few seconds finding it hard to believe that I was home. The front door opened and out rushed a tearful but extremely happy Ann. We hugged and kissed. I told her about my journey from London in this new car. As I walked into the house a sleepy yellow Labrador puppy came plodding toward me!

"What's this!" I cried out.

"I hope you're not going to be cross, but we have talked about getting a dog for ages, and now that daddy and mummy have retired and moved to Lytham, daddy says that he will look after him whilst we are at work, and the exercise will do him good. Do say you're happy. He's a precious poppet and is only twelve weeks old and he has had his vaccinations and can now go for walks and everything," she rambled, her voice filled with mixed emotion.

"Hey, hey! Calm down! Calm down! Come here and give me a hug."

In our hug position we both bent our knees to get nearer to the beautiful puppy who was so excited that he was squirting wee all over the place.

"Ann. It's a bit of a shock BUT I love him. What's he called?"

"Well I've only had him two weeks and daddy thought it would be nice if you and I chose his name together. What do you think?" she said.

I picked this adorable creature up and held him away from me with arms outstretched.

"Look at the size of his feet! He's going to be a big lad. How about... Samson?"

"That's brilliant. It just suits him!" she enthused.

So Samson it was. He was our best pal for some twelve years and was our baby. When we were away Ann's parents happily looked after him and we took him regularly to a self catering cottage in the Lake District for "his" holidays.

Ann had made my favourite meal of chilli con carne with garlic bread and had splashed out on the treat of a bottle of affordable Tonino red wine. It cost 99 pence and was our once a month treat.

Money had been very tight for us for a time, and whilst I had been away my bank, The Midland, had been "onto" Ann in quite an aggressive way about our overdraft facility being exceeded, which upset her greatly. She had phoned Vincent who established that my monthly salary credit had been a day late due to an administrative blip at London office. I could have killed the bank employee for upsetting her for the sake of a few quid, but I suppose he had his job to do.

During the meal Ann said that Vincent had been on the phone saying that I could have the next day off, but could I call at a household claim in Blackpool as nobody else was free to do it!

Apparently the Manchester office had been really busy and Vince wanted me to be forewarned that quite a lot of my existing non-urgent work was as I had left it on my desk three months ago, as none of the lads had had time to deal with it.

"That's bloody marvellous!" I said in a put on cross voice remembering with a smile my first few days of "work" in Cyprus.... gardening!

We laughed at my sarcasm and at the same time realised that Samson was not in the room. We found him in the kitchen chewing the wall!

"Hey what are you doing. Stop it Sam!" I shouted.

"He's been doing this for a few days now. It started with the wallpaper but now he's progressed to the plasterwork," said Ann, accepting the situation as normal puppy behaviour.

"Yeah and it looks like he's had part of the architrave for dessert!" I laughingly replied.

He suddenly abandoned his efforts to demolish the wall and totally oblivious of us, and as fast as his little legs would carry him, raced out of the kitchen through the lounge and into the hall where he immediately launched an unprovoked attack on our front door draught excluder, which was designed in the form of a very long-bodied poodle. He shook it with venom and we stood there laughing at our new pal. He was such a character.

After three minutes of full on assault he suddenly stopped and lay there panting with a big, Labrador puppy, smiley face.

"Time for bed my friend," I said, as I picked him up and, together with Ann, took him into the back garden for his last wee of the day.

I couldn't resist a last look out of the lounge window at the Capri and thereafter plonked Samson in a corner of the kitchen onto his bed of old bath towels. He started to whimper.

"He isn't happy when I leave him at night, so daddy suggested a hot water bottle and a ticking clock for company. It works to an extent but last night I sat with him for about an hour until he got off to sleep," explained Ann.

"I read somewhere that the things you have placed near him are great but some quiet music as well often helps to settle a young pup. I'll go and get a cassette and the cassette recorder." I said.

I came back into the kitchen as Ann placed the hot water bottle and ticking clock, a Big Ben Repeater with the mighty alarm switched "off", beside him. I had selected an Elton John cassette and, after placing it in our portable player, I pressed the "Play" button,

"Daniel is travelling tonight on a plane.
I can see the red tail lights heading for Spay ay ay ain
Oh and I can see Daniel waving goodbye
God it looks like Daniel must be the clouds in my eyes."

On the word "eyes" we realised that Elton's beautiful melody, together with Bernie's brilliant lyrics, had sent Samson into a deep sleep. "Daniel" became Samson's song.

With the beast at rest I picked up the cassette player and said to my lovely wife,

"Come on, I think it's time for bed."

I had slipped my pirated Cyprus-made cassette of my favourite choices from Roger and Alison's record collection into my pocket when I had arrived home.

I knew that the first track was Mozart's Ave, verum corpus, you know the one I thought would make great background music for gentle love making, and swapped the cassettes.

As we walked upstairs I said to Ann, "Have you ever heard a piece of music by Mozart called Ave, verum corpus?"

"I don't think so. Why?"she said, looking puzzled.

"Well I think you're going to like it!"